# ANOTHER BUNCH
# OF FLOWERS

## SHEILA ADBY

Troubador Publishing Ltd
Unit E2 Airfield Business Park,
Harrison Road, Market Harborough,
Leicestershire LE16 7UL
Tel: 0116 279 2299
Email: books@troubador.co.uk
Web: www.troubador.co.uk

ISBN 978-1-80514-412-0

British Library Cataloguing in Publication Data.
A catalogue record for this book is available from the British Library.

Printed and bound in Great Britain by 4edge Limited
Typeset in 11pt Minion Pro by Troubador Publishing Ltd, Leicester, UK

For Mum – I will always remember you,
even if you don't remember me

♥

# ONE

'It seems strange going to the flower club tonight and not being on the committee, doesn't it?' asked Sarah as she drove herself and Polly to the church hall.

'We can just enjoy the evening without being bossed around by Edna.'

'Yeah, it's great,' replied Polly, carefully nursing a plate of home-baked chocolate brownies on her lap.

'I think it's very good of you baking cakes for the meeting tonight after everything that went on at the last committee meeting.'

'If I say I'll do something I always do it. There's no way I'd let our members down, but if Edna is rude to me she's likely to get this plate of cakes in her face,' replied Polly with a wry smile.

Polly and Sarah had both been on the flower club committee for a number of years and Polly had recently decided it was time to step down. Her decision to leave was not taken particularly well by some of the other committee members, least of all Edna, the club chairwoman. In fact, the whole evening had ended up in a terrible argument and resulted in Sarah resigning too.

'I'm disappointed in you,' Edna had snapped.

'Well, I'm sorry about that, Edna, but I work full time and have better things to do with my spare time than attend all these meetings.'

Polly's partner, Mark, had been thrilled when she'd announced to him that she planned on leaving. 'You've been saying that for some time.'

'I know, but I mean it this time. I need a break,' replied Polly.

'Well, don't let Edna bully you into staying. You know what she's like,' warned Mark.

Polly was only too well aware of Edna's bossy and, at times, bullying personality.

'I feel that everyone should come off the committee after a few years. It's ridiculous to me that committee members can stay forever. It's hardly surprising we can't get any new young members. We've got to keep up with the times,' Polly had told the committee at that last meeting.

'If we came off the committee after a few years we would never find anyone who wanted to replace us,' interrupted Barbara, who had herself been on the committee for close to thirty years.

'That may not be the case,' insisted Polly. 'I suspect a number of members are intimidated by the fact that some people have been on this committee since the Stone Age.'

'Well, not quite as long as that,' Barbara bristled, failing to see the funny side of Polly's comment. She might be elderly, but she wasn't that old, yet.

Lizzy sniggered at the prospect of a good fight.

'Won't you reconsider, Polly?' pleaded Rose. 'We love having you on the committee. You've got such great energy and enthusiasm.'

'Well, I'm afraid my enthusiasm is waning right now. I'm tired. I'm busy at work and I want to leave.'

'If that's the way you want to be about it then just go,' snapped Edna.

Everyone looked at her.

'I don't think that was called for,' admonished Sarah. She wasn't going to have her best friend spoken to in such a manner. 'If that's how you feel after everything Polly has done for this club over the last five years then I'm standing down too. I don't want to be on a committee that speaks to members in that way.' She glared at Edna.

'Don't be like that,' replied April, aware that Sarah rarely got angry. 'We don't want to lose either of you.'

The doorbell interrupted their argument. Edna got up and opened the door while everyone sat in silence. In walked Freda who was very late for the meeting, having spent the last hour trying to coax her beloved cat down from her neighbour's tree.

'Sorry I'm late. I just couldn't leave Miss Tilly in the tree. I would worry about her all evening as she's not very streetwise. Did I miss anything?'

'Polly's resigned. Edna was rude to her and now Sarah has resigned,' announced Lizzy recalling the proceedings of the evening and clearly relishing every moment. This would give her something to gossip about.

'Oh.' Freda, unsure how to react to the situation, looked at Edna and then at Polly and could see there was no love between them.

'Yes. Thank you, Lizzy,' Edna spat out the words, clearly annoyed about everything.

'I don't appreciate being spoken to in that tone, Edna.'

Edna ignored her, not wanting to be dragged any further into this argument or have more people resign on her watch.

She took a deep breath.

'Shall we get on?' She glanced at the next item on the agenda. 'Treasurer's report. Barbara?'

Barbara, somewhat flustered, quickly flicked through her notebook. She trembled, realising all eyes were on her. 'Um,' she stuttered. 'Sorry, ladies, I think I've left the piece of paper at home, the one with the details on.'

Polly tutted as Barbara pulled out a handful of paper scraps.

'What's your problem, Polly?' Edna glared at her.

'Only that I've been saying for years we should automate our accounts.'

'Not this again. Anyway, as you're stepping down it's not your business, is it?' Polly's mouth dropped open, but no words came out.

'Next item, charity event. Rose, over to you.' Edna wasn't too sure what this meant and wasn't particularly interested after the evening's turn of events, but she felt that as chairwoman she should find out what Rose was getting up to.

'I've arranged to have a table at a charity event next month.' informed Rose, hoping that the change in subject might calm everyone down. 'I do hope some of you will come along. I thought we could promote the club and perhaps make a few flower arrangements to sell.'

Edna felt rather angry that once again Rose had gone ahead and arranged a charity event without consulting her, but in view of the icy atmosphere in the room she didn't dare challenge her.

'That's a lovely idea,' she forced out the words.

Rose glanced around the table at the other committee members to see if she could get any support for the event. Polly and Sarah were still seething and couldn't even look at her; Barbara and Freda were looking somewhat embarrassed; and Lizzy was lapping it all up.

'Err, OK,' she stuttered, aware that perhaps tonight wasn't the best time to try and rally support. 'If anyone does decide they would like to come and help that would be great.'

'Thank you, Rose. Is there any other business?' Edna tried to avoid eye contact with anyone and kept glancing at the agenda in front of her on the table. She was greeted with silence.

'Well in that case I'm going to put the kettle on and get us all a slice of cake.' She quickly headed out to the kitchen and was relieved not to be in the room anymore.

Barbara rushed out behind her. 'I'll help,' she offered, knowing full well that Edna didn't need any help, but she didn't want to find herself in a difficult position with Polly and Sarah.

Ordinarily the very mention of a slice of cake would have got Polly's attention, but not after everything that had been said this evening. She had well and truly lost her appetite.

This had all happened a couple of weeks ago and since then there had been no contact from the committee, so Polly and Sarah weren't too sure what type of reception they would get this evening.

It had begun to drizzle rain. Sarah parked close to the hall so that Polly didn't have to walk too far with her tray of cakes.

It had been threatening to rain all day but had obviously been waiting to start at the most inconvenient time.

At the hall they were greeted by Barbara and Freda at the reception desk.

A voice accompanied the approaching clattering of heels. 'Can I interest you in a raffle ticket, ladies?' Julia had been filled in on what had happened at the committee meeting. She'd been away on one of her 'mini-breaks' and missed all the excitement.

Sarah pulled out her purse to buy some tickets as Polly went to place her cakes on the nearby cake table. In front of her were lots of cakes, positioned in an interesting pattern that Edna had obviously spent a lot of time arranging to the best effect. Edna spotted her and rushed over.

'Hello, Polly,' she said, coldly. 'Why have you made cakes this evening?'

'My name was on the rota.' Polly was somewhat taken aback by Edna's question.

'I assumed that you wouldn't be making any after your behaviour the other evening, so I made extra.' She waved her clipboard in Polly's face.

Polly glared. This was like a red rag to a bull.

'How dare you say that. I wasn't the one out of order. All I did was resign.'

Edna ignored her.

'Well, it's too bad that you've wasted your time baking, Edna, cos I've made more than enough for all our members.' Polly spat the words. She edged her plate of brownies up against the ones which Edna had already placed there and tried to nudge them along so her cake plate would fit.

Edna was furious. No one touched her cake table when she had spent an age setting it up.

'*You* may put your cakes over there.' She pointed an authoritative finger towards a table a few feet away. She was hoping to diffuse the situation and she didn't want a scene, especially as the area chairwoman was due to arrive at any moment.

'No, I will not.' Polly's voice was getting louder. '*These* are going on the cake table.'

'Oh, no, they're not.' Edna took hold of the cake plate that Polly was holding. 'Let go,' she ordered.

'No.' Polly held on tightly. In a split second the two of them were having a tug of war with the plate.

'Edna, please!' Freda tried to interrupt.

Edna glanced over her shoulder and noticed that Cynthia, the area chairwoman, was standing behind her. She lost concentration and as she did Polly gave a strong tug of the plate and freed it from Edna's grasp. The cakes flipped off the plate. Some ended up on top of Edna's pineapple upside-down cake, and others were strewn across the floor or down the front of Polly's new white blouse.

'Now look what you've done. Get this mess cleared up.' Edna turned around to face Cynthia.

Cynthia's bemused look gave away that she had expected to come for an evening of fun and flowers, not step into a cake war.

'I'm so sorry about that,' Edna stuttered as she took Cynthia by the elbow and led her to another part of the hall.

Cynthia glanced over her shoulder and saw Polly welling up with tears of anger as she wiped away the chocolate brownies that had stuck themselves to her blouse.

Cynthia smiled inwardly, recalling the last time she had seen Polly. It had been a couple of years earlier at an area flower show and Polly's exhibit had ended up in a heap on the floor. This event had left a lasting impression on Cynthia. Polly clearly seemed to attract trouble.

Sarah and Lizzy rushed over to help Polly clear up the mess.

'Let's leave,' suggested Sarah. 'This is the last straw.'

'I'm going to stay just to spite her,' said Polly, defiantly. 'I'm going to let everyone see what a bully Edna is.'

Sarah and Lizzy looked at each other, unsure whether this was a good idea or not.

Polly's long-time friend, Maggie, arrived while the clean-up job was underway, and Polly was sponging down her new blouse.

'What on earth happened?' she asked, curious as to all the commotion.

'Edna wouldn't let me put my cakes on the table. We had a fight and I lost. How petty can anyone be?'

'I heard that things were tense between you two, but I didn't realise they were this bad.'

'Who told you there was a problem?' Polly was curious as to who had been discussing committee issues away from the meeting as she certainly hadn't.

'I think Jennifer told me. No idea where she heard it. She said you'd stormed out of the committee meeting.'

'No, I didn't. Why would she say that?' Polly was shocked that the grapevine was clearly not working particularly well on this occasion.

'You know what it's like with rumours. Can never trust them.' Maggie kicked herself, afraid that she might have made matters worse, and wishing that she hadn't let on that she had heard anything.

Sarah and Polly simultaneously looked at Lizzy, who, in their eyes, was probably the culprit for spreading these rumours.

'What? Well, I might have mentioned it to someone. But I don't remember saying you walked out. I just said that things got a bit tense,' Lizzy insisted.

Polly wasn't sure whether or not to believe her. She was a renowned gossip but she didn't want to fall out with her as well. Right now she needed all the support she could get.

Edna was hoping to impress Cynthia with the flower club she had been the chairwoman of for the past seven years, but after witnessing the skirmish with Polly any hope of this had long gone.

Cynthia was shown to her seat in the front row whilst Edna prepared herself for making all the club announcements. By chance there were a couple of empty seats next to Cynthia so Sarah and Polly decided to occupy these. When they were on the committee they tended not to sit in the front row, even though there was an unwritten rule that the committee members always sat there. Polly and Sarah didn't want to appear as though they were receiving preferential treatment, but now they were no longer on the committee they decided to sit there as a further act of defiance against Edna.

Edna glanced over the top of the reading glasses she had perched on the end of her nose and noticed them sitting in the front row. She glared.

'Ladies, can we begin?' Edna shouted over the chit-chat in the hall. Almost immediately the hall fell to silence with no one daring to speak over her. Whispers of the cake incident were spreading fast.

The demonstration that evening was nothing to get excited about. Whether it was because the area chairwoman was sitting in the front row, or the fact that Polly was sitting next to her covered in chocolate, the demonstrator seemed to be distracted and several of her designs didn't go according to plan. One exhibit fell out of its container as it was top heavy and hadn't been firmly secured. For the next five minutes, although it seemed considerably longer, the demonstrator stood with her back to the audience as she tried to rescue the arrangement. Everyone started mumbling. Sarah started sniggering which soon got Polly started.

'All I can see is her bum,' she whispered to her.

Polly couldn't answer. It was clear that the events of the evening were starting to take their toll. Polly desperately tried to contain her laughter but as her stresses released themselves, she lost control.

Maggie was sitting behind them. 'Trust you two,' she hissed, well aware that when Polly and Sarah started laughing it was hard to stop them. Sarah turned round to look at her, tears of laughter in her eyes.

While the rescue mission was in full flow, Edna headed to the stage to offer her help. The demonstrator wasn't the tidiest person in the world and had piled all her waste beside her turntable. It was beginning to infuriate Edna, who, by now, was on a short fuse.

She started tidying up, despite the demonstrator's protestations. She gathered up the wrappings from several bunches of flowers and all the debris and threw them in the bin bag nearby. The situation made Sarah and Polly laugh even more as they had visions of Edna and the demonstrator having a tug of war over the rubbish. Edna glanced up and noticed they were laughing at her, along with the majority of people in the room. Even Cynthia had given up trying to stifle her laughter by then. Edna turned away, afraid of what she might say out loud, and headed back to her seat.

No sooner had she settled back down than there was a rattling on the door as someone tried to get into the hall. Edna mouthed to Freda to go and open the door. Freda tiptoed to the doorway and tried to open the door as quietly as she could, but something was blocking the door. Some idiot had placed a chair on the other side of it.

Audrey, aware that she was running late, desperately tried to squeeze through the narrow gap and somehow she became wedged. Freda tried to push her back out and open the other door, but as she did this Audrey disappeared. By then all eyes were on Freda, who looked at Edna and couldn't stop laughing.

Edna mouthed to her, 'Where's she gone?' to which Freda shrugged her shoulders. At that moment, Audrey, having decided that it may be better to come in via the back door, appeared from the back of the stage.

Polly started laughing. It was good to let off a bit of steam after the earlier shenanigans. It was all the more hilarious as Edna clearly didn't see the funny side of it.

Once the commotion settled the demonstrator completed her third design and it was time for the tea break. Everyone got up rapidly and headed to the cake table to see what tasty cakes were on offer. Some of Polly's cakes looked decidedly battered, but nevertheless still deliciously appetising. Edna was determined that everyone should try her cakes and she hovered by the cake table encouraging people to choose hers, as though this was some sort of competitive battle.

Polly was gasping for a cup of tea but didn't think she was up to more confrontation with Edna, so Maggie volunteered to get her something to drink. 'Fancy a piece of cake with that?' she asked, slightly sheepishly.

'I'll have one of mine, thanks. If I eat one of Edna's cakes, I'm likely to choke on it.' Maggie smiled and headed off to join the queue. She returned a short time later with a cup of tea. 'No cake, I'm afraid. All yours have gone.'

Polly felt a little disappointed as she was in desperate need of a rich chocolate brownie, but secretly pleased that her cakes went first, leaving Edna with half a plate of brownie-spattered pineapple upside-down cakes to take home.

With the tea break over, the demonstrator tried to pick up where she had left off. The second half of her demonstration was more or less the same as the first with similar designs and another accumulation of waste which was clearly infuriating Edna, who refrained from saying anything and felt relieved when the evening was over.

As Polly was gathering up her belongings at the end of the evening Cynthia leant over to her.

'Polly, there's no way you should've been spoken to in that manner.' Cynthia had been thinking about the incident during the demonstration.

'I know. All I did was bring some cakes along for our members. Quite honestly with behaviour like this I feel like quitting flowers altogether.'

'Please don't do that. You love flowers and do some amazing work. It's just that you've encountered some difficult personalities.' Cynthia could relate to Polly as she too had had some issues several years earlier. 'Why don't you have a go at running your own flower club?' she suggested.

'Really? I can't say I've ever thought about doing something like that.'

'Well do give it some thought. You'd be great at it.'

Polly left the hall whilst thinking over what Cynthia had said. Sarah could sense that Polly was scheming something.

'I wonder if I could start up my own club,' she muttered to herself.

'What's that?' asked Sarah.

'Nothing. Just thinking out loud.'

They drove in silence to Polly's house, both deep in thought.

'Don't let Edna get to you,' Sarah tried to offer comfort, 'she's such a bully.'

'Don't worry, I won't,' insisted Polly. She got out of the car and rushed up the path to avoid getting too wet. The earlier drizzle was now coming down thick and fast.

Mark, who had been enjoying a quiet night in, was startled by Polly's sudden appearance in the hallway, most of all by the fact that her top was covered in a chocolate stain.

'You'll never guess what happened,' she blurted out.

'Did you trip over or something?'

'No?' Polly was surprised by the question.

'Then why have you got chocolate all down the front of your blouse?'

'Cynthia told me to start up a new flower club. I might just do that,' she said, totally ignoring Mark's question.

'How does that link in with all the chocolate on your blouse?'

Polly glanced down and realised that she looked a fright.

'Edna refused to let me put my cakes on the table with hers, so we had a tug of war. She let go and I ended up with brownie all over me.'

Mark stared at her, wide-eyed with disbelief.

'What do you mean she wouldn't let you put your cakes on the table?'

'You know how she is.' Polly shrugged. 'She always has to call the shots. Well not this time. How dare she behave like that. If she thinks she's going to get away with this she's got another thing coming.'

# TWO

'If she thinks she's coming back on the committee at any stage she can think again.' Edna was well and truly in a strop as she stomped around the kitchen getting her breakfast.

'Perhaps she won't want to,' replied George, wearily. Edna's long-suffering husband had put up with her incessant tossing and turning all night.

Edna glared at him. In her opinion everyone should feel privileged to stand as a committee member.

'Anyway, don't your members vote for people?' he mused, trying to make sense of the situation.

'Yes.'

'So, in actual fact it isn't your decision. If she gets nominated and voted in there's nothing you can do.'

'Are you taking her side?'

'No. Just stating the facts.'

Edna thought for a moment. George had a point.

'Well, let's hope it doesn't come to that.'

Cynthia awoke with a smile. The memory of the cake fight at the flower club the previous evening fresh in her mind. Why on earth two women would end up fighting over a plate of cakes was beyond her comprehension. Seeing Polly end up with chocolate brownies stuck to her clothing took her mind back to the first time she met Polly. Whoever thought flower arranging could be so dramatic.

As part of her duties at the area flower show she patrolled the marquee, checking that all the exhibitors were getting on with setting up their designs without problems and without cheating. Having popped out of the marquee just long enough for a quick cup of tea she returned to total mayhem and three exhibits lying in a heap on the floor. Some exhibitors were stomping around, others were in tears and Polly was buried under a pile of flowers and floral foam. There was never any proof of sabotage, despite Polly's insistence that fellow competitor, Amy, had deliberately tampered with her design, but nevertheless Cynthia had to step in and calm the situation down.

Aware of the big recruitment drive to encourage more people to take up flower arranging and join a flower club, Cynthia felt dismayed after witnessing such an incident the previous night. She decided she'd phone Polly to offer her some encouragement to try and set up a new club.

By the time Mark had rallied and arrived in the kitchen in the hope of grabbing a quick breakfast before he headed to work, Polly had her blouse soaking in the sink. The smell of detergent was enough to put him off any food that morning.

'Look,' she said, tearfully, holding up the dripping blouse with the distinctive brown stain on it.

'Have you tried bleach?' asked Mark, tentatively, almost afraid to make the suggestion, although judging by the smell of chemicals he suspected Polly had tried pretty much everything.

'Yep. I've also tried this new super-duper detergent that is supposed to remove any stain known to mankind. Still hasn't worked.'

'I can't believe that two women could end up having a tug of war over a plate of cakes.' Mark, seeing the funny side of the situation, did his best to try to stifle his laughter. Polly, standing with her back to him, sensed that he was secretly laughing at her. She turned to face him. The sight of Mark made her burst out laughing.

'I thought this flower arranging lark was supposed to be fun.' Mark had been amazed by some of Polly's stories over the years about what went on at flower club. 'You could write a book about it.'

'I might just do that,' mused Polly. 'Perhaps one day. You're right – it is supposed to be fun. Anyone would've thought that I'd done something terribly wrong, not just baked a load of cakes. That woman will be the death of me.'

The phone ringing interrupted them. She didn't recognise the voice immediately.

'Polly?'

'Yes.'

'It's Cynthia.' There was a momentary pause. 'Area Chairwoman.'

'Oh, hello Cynthia,' acknowledged Polly once the penny had dropped.

'Just following up on the incident last night and our conversation. I hoped to catch you before you went out.' Polly wondered why the area chairwoman would be phoning her, especially so early in the morning. 'I just wanted to reiterate

17

that I think you should give serious consideration to setting up your own flower club.'

'Can't say I'd ever thought about it before.'

'Fact is that we need to encourage young people to take up flower arranging. Membership figures are dropping all the time and some clubs are closing down due to lack of support. We need to encourage people like you to take an active part in the future of flower clubs.'

No one had ever suggested anything like this to Polly before. 'No idea where to begin,' she stuttered, taken aback by Cynthia's confidence in her.

'Just get a group of friends together, find somewhere to meet and then place a local advert. Don't think really big at this stage – it doesn't matter if you only get a handful of people together. As long as you aren't out of pocket you can build the club through word of mouth.'

'I'll think about it,' hesitated Polly, which seemed to satisfy Cynthia.

Mark looked at her. 'What are you thinking about?'

'Setting up a new flower club.'

'Oh that. I thought you were joking last night. Don't you think you've got enough going on at the moment? After all, the main reason you quit the committee was that you were too busy. Now you're thinking of taking on even more work.'

'I know. But at least this will be my club. I'll call the shots and won't have Edna bossing me around and telling me when I can bake cakes.'

'Suppose so. Just give it some thought before you jump in with both feet.' Mark, knowing he was fighting a losing battle, set off for work.

# THREE

'This is all very exciting,' enthused Lizzy when she met up with Polly and Sarah at the local tea room. 'I feel like I'm on some sort of covert mission.'

Maggie arrived shortly afterwards, followed by Rose. As they headed to their reserved seats in the corner they ogled the array of cakes at the counter.

The waitress headed over to take their order. 'Would you like a piece of cake?' she enquired, although had she known Polly, she would have realised this was quite a stupid question as cake was rarely something Polly refused.

'What cakes have you got?' enquired Polly, knowing full well what was on offer as she had scrutinised them on arrival. She was hoping to buy herself a bit of time whilst she decided which one to choose.

'Carrot cake, chocolate fudge cake, tea loaf, sticky ginger cake, flapjack or macaroon,' the waitress reeled off.

'I think I'm going to try your sticky ginger cake,' replied Polly. 'Sounds quite delicious.'

Maggie leaned forward over the table. 'So, Polly, what's

this all about?' Curious as to why Polly had suddenly called them all together.

'What would you say if I said I was going to start my own flower club?' asked Polly, trying to gauge the reaction of her friends.

'I, for one, think that's a brilliant idea,' agreed Maggie.

Lizzy looked a little disappointed. 'I thought you had some big announcement. Like you'd won the lottery or something.'

Everyone smiled. 'Trust you to be disappointed,' laughed Rose.

'I was just hoping for some earth-shattering news.'

'Well, it is really. Polly will be taking on Edna,' pointed out Sarah, mischievously.

'Too right. I'll show her.' Polly was full of fighting talk.

'So how do you go about setting up a new club?' Maggie was totally bemused as to how you would even begin.

'That's why I've asked you guys here today. I've absolutely no idea!'

'But Cynthia gave you some ideas,' reminded Sarah.

'What? Cynthia, the area chairman?' Rose wasn't aware that she and Polly knew each other.

'Yes. She came up to me at the end of the club meeting and suggested I set up a new flower club.'

'How d'you know her?' asked Rose.

'Remember the sabotage incident a couple of years ago when my design toppled at the area show?'

'And your flying sphere that took out two of the exhibits,' reminded Sarah.

'How could we forget,' laughed Maggie, whose exhibit would have been wiped out by the flying sphere had it not been for some quick thinking on her part.

'Cynthia was part of the show committee. She is the person who negotiated the extra half hour for me to set up my design.'

Sarah started to laugh. 'Wonder what she makes of you. The first time you met you were under a pile of flowers and wet foam with chaos all around you. The second time you met you're under a pile of chocolate brownies.'

Polly laughed. 'You're right. I hadn't thought of it like that. I'm not sure I made the right impression on her.'

'She probably thinks that you're a walking disaster,' stated Lizzy without giving much thought to what she was saying.

Sarah glanced at her.

'Sorry, did I say that out loud?'

Polly giggled. 'At least you've the nerve to say what everyone else is thinking.'

The waitress, interrupting their conversation, placed the various mugs of tea and coffee on the table and tried to remember who had ordered what cake. Polly looked longingly at the piece of sticky ginger cake in front of her. Unable to resist any longer, she took a bite. She sat back in her chair, a look of ecstasy on her face. It really was delicious.

Lizzy started laughing. 'Enjoying that, Polly?'

'Mmm, oh yes,' she replied, licking her lips.

'Shall we continue?' urged Rose, dying to know what Polly's plan of action was.

'Sorry about that. It was yummy. I just couldn't resist. Where were we?' Polly had completely lost her train of thought.

'You were telling us that Cynthia had discussed this with you,' Rose reminded her, bringing the conversation back on track. 'What sort of things did she say?'

'Not much, other than all we need is a hall and a few people to start with, then build the club from there.'

'I like the mention of "we". A minute ago you said you were going to start up a club. Suddenly it's the royal "we".' Maggie wasn't sure she wanted the hassle of setting up a new club.

'I'll need your help with this. I've no idea how to get things up and running.'

'Let's make a list of what we need.' Sarah liked to keep lists of everything in her life. Without her lists she was lost.

She pulled out a notebook from her handbag and sat poised with a pen. She nodded to Polly to continue.

'First off, we need to decide a day and time for this club. The fact is that more people are having to work later into life, or those who have retired are often stuck looking after grandkids.'

'So, are we looking at an evening or weekend club?' asked Maggie.

'I think so.'

'In all honesty when I get home from work some nights I feel so exhausted I don't fancy turning out again, especially in the bad weather,' admitted Sarah.

'Know what you mean. In that case, how about a Saturday morning club? We could meet from ten until twelve once a month.'

Sarah quickly scribbled this down.

'Next question is the venue. Where can the club meet?'

'It has to be somewhere central so that if someone doesn't have a car they can still get there.' Rose made a valid point.

'It would be good if it was near a supermarket too as I suspect a lot of people would do their shopping on a Saturday. This way they can combine the two,' suggested Lizzy.

Polly wasn't sure if she understood Lizzy's logic, but at this point she wasn't going to discount anything that was suggested.

'What do we do about money? These halls aren't exactly cheap to hire,' Maggie pointed out.

'What about demonstrators? Where will the money come from to pay for them?' Lizzy chipped in with her concerns.

Sarah's list was starting to take shape albeit full of questions.

'I'm not sure. I think we need a totally different approach from other flower clubs.'

'What do you mean by that?' Rose questioned Polly's suggestion.

'Perhaps we need to ask ourselves the question of what we hope to achieve.' Sarah was clearly on the same wavelength as Polly.

Everyone looked blankly at her.

'Is this a club that is all about flowers? Or is this a club that is about people who have a common interest in flowers?' she continued.

'What, make it more of a social club that happens to like flowers?' Rose was warming to the idea.

'Exactly, Rose. Focus on creating a friendly, sociable group who meet up once a month for a cup of tea, a slice of cake and a chat and while they are there they can make a flower arrangement or watch someone giving a demonstration.'

'That way we wouldn't be in competition with Edna's flower club,' Maggie chimed in.

Polly pulled a face.

'I know you want to get back at Edna, but if we compete with her we'll end up flat on our faces. At least if we set up a club that can run alongside it we might attract some of her members too,' Maggie tried to reason with her. The last thing she wanted was to get embroiled in their disagreement.

Polly was slightly disappointed. She was determined to show Edna that she could do a better job, but perhaps Maggie had a point.

'We could have some craft sessions too,' suggested Maggie, trying to change the subject. 'I'd be happy to run some of those.' Everyone knew that Maggie could make pretty much anything.

'Polly, you'd be great at demonstrating or running the workshops and once we get the club up and running we might be able to afford to pay someone to come along and host some of the meetings.' Rose too hoped to steer Polly away from a vendetta. She hated confrontational situations at the best of times.

'I like the fact that you're now including yourself in "we"!' Polly's eyes lit up realising she wasn't alone in her quest.

'We assumed that you're not going to let us off the hook that easily! I'm happy to help you with whatever I can,' volunteered Maggie, having had a change of heart.

'That's great.'

'So, what we need right now is a cheap venue that is available on a Saturday morning.' Sarah tried to steer the conversation back on track.

'Don't you run workshops in a hall near here, Polly?' asked Lizzy.

'Only a few times a year. The hall is cheap, but it's always booked out by the Magic Circle on a Saturday morning. So that's out. There's no way we'd get them to change. I can't even get them out of the hall when I'm running my workshop. They hang around for ages, gassing.'

'They say women can talk. I'm sure men are far worse when they get started.'

'Don't they help you with all your stuff?' Rose was sure that there were still some chivalrous men around.

'No. They watch me and make idiotic comments like, "Ooh you've got a lot of flowers." One time when I was unloading the car I slipped on the mud and actually slid under my car. They were all standing around gawking with their mouths open. No one came to help. Of course, they made a snide comment when I got back on my feet.'

Everyone stared at her in disbelief.

'What, they didn't even come to your rescue?' enquired Lizzy.

'Nope.' Polly began pondering, the memory of the incident still very clear in her mind.

'That's a shame. Let's have a think about the venue and see what we can come up with. Next issue. How do we attract members? And in particular young people? I see this club as being one for people who go out to work, rather than retired folk.'

'But you're not going to exclude anyone, are you? If someone wants to join we should never turn them away. I think we'd be hard-pressed for members anyway, but we do need to focus on finding younger members.' Rose was concerned Polly might have a blacklist.

'What about us going into schools or colleges to talk about flowers?'

'That's an idea, although I'm not sure if we'd drum up much interest. Also, we'd have to charge people either an annual membership or monthly fee so the question is would students have any money to pay for this?'

'Perhaps we're getting ahead of ourselves. Perhaps we need to find a small hall that we can hire cheaply. Then have an open morning. That way we can gauge interest.' Rose always came up with a sensible idea.

'We could leaflet the area and put up some posters in the library and supermarkets,' Lizzy suggested.

'Why don't we fix a date in a few weeks' time and work on that?' Sarah always liked to have a level of control over her life. Apart from her lists, her diary was her next best friend and she never left home without it.

The waitress came over to the table, aware that Polly and the others had been sitting there for some considerable length of time.

'Would you like anything else?' she enquired.

'I, for one, could do with another cup of tea while we finish this list off,' admitted Polly. And of course, no cup of tea is complete without a slice of cake.

# FOUR

Polly eagerly opened the brown envelope that had arrived that morning. Not that the envelope looked remotely exciting, but she recognised the handwriting and knew that this would contain the show schedule for the forthcoming local horticultural show. This was a show that anyone who's anyone in her town competed in and, judging by previous years, it was taken very seriously.

This year the schedule was printed on rather bland-looking pink paper and on this occasion, it was attached to a letter. The letter was from Gordon, the organiser of the event.

Mark noticed Polly scrutinising the letter. 'What's up?'

Polly continued to read, then looked up at him. 'It's from Gordon.' Mark looked at her blankly. He had absolutely no idea who she was talking about.

'You know Gordon. You do. He arranges the horticultural show.'

This still didn't mean anything to him. 'Why's he written to you?'

'He's asked me if I'll judge the flower arrangements in the show.'

Mark started to laugh.

Polly looked at him. 'What's so funny?'

'Well, that should take you all of two minutes. There are only ever one or two exhibits in each class. Even I could judge them.'

Polly had thought it quite an honour to be invited to do the judging, but Mark had quickly burst her bubble and brought her down to earth. 'Suppose you're right. Last year they were dreadful. A child who was blindfolded and had one hand tied behind their back could have done better. Edna's was the only decent arrangement there. No wonder she wins the trophy every year.'

Just as Polly was finishing her sentence the realisation hit her. If Edna was competing, then Polly knew she definitely wanted to be the judge.

'Aren't you supposed to be setting up a new flower club?' Mark had changed the subject, well aware that Polly was daydreaming of vengeance.

'Oh yes.'

'No need to sound so enthusiastic,' he said sarcastically.

'I'm just wondering if I've bitten off more than I can chew. What do I know about setting up a flower club?'

'I'm sure you'll be great at it. You're good at organising things.' Despite being totally against the idea in the beginning he knew that Polly really needed his support rather than his negativity. If she took on too much, he'd rather she realised it without him continually pointing it out to her.

'I need to find a hall that is cheap and available on a Saturday.'

'What about the church hall?'

'Where Edna's flower club meets?'

'Yes. Like the way you refer to it as Edna's flower club now!'

Polly knew the vicar and was aware that he always kept the rent low. She just wondered if he would be happy to hire her the hall knowing it was for another flower club. Edna and him had been friends for donkeys years so there might be some loyalty issues with that one.

'I'll give him a call. What's the worst that can happen?'

Polly picked up her address book and proceeded to dial the number for the hall. The phone was quickly answered, almost as though the vicar was expecting a call from someone.

Polly proceeded to explain to him what she wanted to do and why she wanted the hall. She hardly left space for the vicar to get a word in edgeways. Eventually, when he saw a chance to speak, he told her that the hall wasn't available, that he had only just rented it to a keep fit club, so unfortunately, he couldn't help. Polly was disappointed but he kindly suggested another hall, not too far from the railway station *and* it might be available on Saturdays.

After a quick call to the caretaker of the railway hall, Polly faced Mark with a huge grin on her face.

'I take it you were successful?'

'Yep! He'll let us have it for twenty-five pounds for the morning. Got to go down there later today and he'll give me a set of keys. Can't wait.'

'That's incredibly cheap. You sure he doesn't mean that's the hourly rate?'

'No. He said it was that for the whole morning.'

'Wonder what's wrong with it?' he grimaced.

Polly started to wonder if Mark could be right. This amount was too good to be true.

'Well, there's only one way to find out. I'm heading over there now. Want to come?'

This was a chance Mark definitely didn't want to miss.

They jumped into the car and in a matter of minutes they were outside the caretaker's house. The elderly man seemed surprised to see Polly on his doorstep so soon after the call. He brushed the cake crumbs from his old cardigan in an attempt to look decent.

'Let me get the keys and I'll show you the place,' he mumbled whilst shuffling slowly down the hallway to pick up one of the sets of keys from a bowl on the hall table.

Polly looked at Mark and pulled a face, trying not to get uptight. She wasn't exactly patient when she wanted someone to do something for her. Eventually the caretaker made his way outside clutching the keys in his hand. They followed him to the hall which was a stone's throw away from his house. He unlocked the heavy padlock on the surrounding fence, and then unlocked the door to the hall.

The hall was very old, albeit a reasonable size. It appeared to be made from corrugated iron and was in dire need of a coat of paint. There was no stage, but there was a pillar in the centre of the room, which seemed quite an odd thing. The hall felt cold and damp. High on the walls were contraptions that Polly and Mark had never seen before. Gas fires had been suspended from the walls.

'What's that?' asked Mark, pointing to the fires.

'That's the heating system.' The caretaker pulled at the metal chain which was hanging down from the heater. The smell of gas filled the room and almost immediately a small naked flame ignited the gas. The heater roared into life and in a short time the hall was feeling extremely hot.

'They're very effective,' said the caretaker, proud of his antiquated heating system.

'Yes they are, but are they safe?' Mark was concerned. In his job he dealt with health and safety issues and wasn't sure that these things would pass any form of safety checks.

'Never had a problem yet. Just remember to pull the chain in the opposite direction to switch them off.'

'What if the pilot light goes out? Surely you'd end up gassing yourself.' Polly agreed with Mark that they didn't appear to be the safest of heaters.

'They've never done it yet,' replied the caretaker, unable to understand why Polly and Mark appeared so worried.

'I'll show you the kitchen.' He shuffled across the hall through a side door into a reasonably sized kitchen that was kitted out with a modern cooker, fridge and hot water boiler. They all seemed to tick the boxes as far as Polly was concerned. There was a serving hatch into the main hall.

'That's handy,' she pointed out to Mark. 'I can put the cakes there.'

'What cakes? I thought this was a flower club, not a baking one.'

'It is, but we must have cake too.'

'So, do you want to rent the hall?' the caretaker asked, slightly abruptly.

'You did say it was twenty-five pounds for the whole morning?'

'Yes, you can have it from nine until twelve-thirty if that's what you want, but you must be out on time as a knitting circle meets here on Saturday afternoons and they won't like to be kept waiting.'

'No problem.' Polly paid over the first month's rent in cash and the caretaker handed her the keys. Polly and Mark drove off as they watched the caretaker slowly shuffling back to his house.

'Not sure I'm happy about those heaters,' stressed Mark.

'Don't worry about it. Not as though we're in there all the time. We might only need to use them a couple of times a year. If I don't get on with them I'll take a couple of halogen heaters in there instead.'

Mark seemed placated by Polly's answer.

'All I've got to do now is get some people along. I need to get some posters up in the supermarkets and libraries to try and rally support.'

'Well, you have a few weeks to garner some interest otherwise you and Sarah are going to rattle around that hall.'

Polly, full of excitement, phoned Sarah, Lizzy, Rose and Maggie with the news about the hall. Her call was greeted with slightly muted responses, with Lizzy stating outright, 'I thought they pulled that place down years ago.'

'It's just what we need for now. It's cheap, it's central and it's got its own car park. Once we get the club established, we can go upmarket.' Polly hoped to convince the others although she wasn't sure they were as enthusiastic about it as she was. She also had a niggling doubt as to whether this whole plan was a good idea.

# FIVE

Having designed a poster for her new flower club and handed them out wherever she could, Polly set about deciding what to bake for the horticultural show as that day was fast approaching.

She scrutinised the schedule. There were a series of baking options for her, including a couple of cake recipes. 'At least this year I'll get it right.'

Mark laughed. A couple of years earlier Polly had picked up a show schedule from a local shop and selected a few of the recipes from the baked goods section. She practised them all week until Mark was sick and tired of trying them. On the day of the show Sarah and Polly headed to the showground. Polly carefully carried in all her baked goods from the car. Sarah remained in the car as she wanted to make a couple of phone calls. When Polly arrived in the hall she stood looking at the baked goods section. Having looked at all the classes, Polly was puzzled.

'Is there a problem?' asked one of the stewards.

'I can't see the classes for my fruit cake, lemon and blueberry loaf and chocolate chip cookies.'

'Ah. Oh dear. I'm afraid that was last year's schedule. This year it's orange and cranberry cookies, pecan pie and chocolate shortbread fingers.'

Polly stared in disbelief. 'I don't believe it.' Just at that moment Edna appeared. She didn't even try to hide her amusement at the situation. 'I'm sorry, Polly. You've baked the wrong things.'

Polly could feel her face burning with embarrassment. She made a quick exit and rushed back to the car. Sarah was taken by surprise at the sudden appearance of Polly opening the boot and chucking the tins in.

'Everything OK?' she asked.

'I only went and baked all the wrong things,' said Polly, crossly. She was furious at herself.

'But they were on the schedule,' insisted Sarah. Having been one of Polly's guinea pigs over the last few weeks, she too had been pretty sick and tired of sampling the lemon and blueberry loaf.

'That's right, but it was the wrong schedule. It was from last year! I'm so embarrassed. I don't want to come back.' Polly revved up the engine and in a split second they had left the showground.

Mark was working at the dining table when Polly arrived home. He looked up from his work and could immediately sense Polly wasn't in the greatest of moods.

'Wasn't expecting to see you for a while.' Polly put the cake tins down. Mark opened one of the tins. 'Why have you brought these back?'

'I've baked all the wrong stuff.' Mark looked puzzled.

'I used the wrong schedule. Bloody annoying. I must have picked up last year's.' Mark, failing to understand Polly's disappointment, helped himself to one of the chocolate chip cookies.

'Looks like I'll have to eat these.'

'Is that all you can say?' sulked Polly, snatching the cookie and throwing it back into the container.

'Edna was there. She laughed at me.'

'Oh dear,' Mark tried to sound sympathetic whilst helping himself to another cookie.

Polly thought back to that moment. There was no way she'd make that mistake again. 'Umm. Think I might have a go at the fruit tart and the carrot cake. Or should I try the muffins and the cheese scones?'

Mark wasn't paying much attention, but the mention of cheese scones was enough for him to put his newspaper down and take note.

'Cheese scones, my favourite.'

'Think I might try all of them and see which is successful.'

'What, like a dress rehearsal?' Mark was already salivating at the thought of it.

'I'll take them into work to get some opinions from my colleagues,' she continued.

'Oh.'

'What?'

'Thought you were going to let me try them.'

'OK, you get to try some too, but you can't eat all of them.'

'Just the cheese scones.'

Polly ignored him. The last time she baked a tray of cheese scones she couldn't believe how many had disappeared when she'd returned to the kitchen.

'Where have all the scones gone?' she asked, wondering if some invisible creature had got into the house to devour them. Mark looked guilty, quickly brushing away crumbs from his mouth and from his lap.

'Um. I might have had one or two,' he sheepishly replied.

'One or two?' screamed Polly. 'I made a baker's dozen and there are only eight left. Tell me you haven't eaten them all.'

He flushed red with embarrassment at having been caught out and the realisation that what started as one scone had quickly escalated to five without even realising. What made matters worse was that Polly swore she could gain a pound or two just by looking at a cake, whereas Mark could consume pretty much everything in sight and not gain an ounce.

Polly knew that she would have to be strict with the number of scones Mark was allowed if she wanted to have any left to exhibit. She headed out into the kitchen to check the ingredients she had in her cupboard, and quickly scribbled a list of the missing items ready to start baking the following day.

'Thought I'd bake tomorrow and take them into the office on Monday.' Polly had been tasked with writing up a disaster recovery plan. No one else offered, so she volunteered. She knew her presentation was going to be pretty boring, so she thought that taking a few cakes in might be a treat.

'Well, that should at least keep their interest if they know there's some home-baked stuff coming their way.' Mark thought it was a good idea.

Polly picked up her handbag and coat. 'Popping out now to get some ingredients ready for the big bake,' she shouted as she headed to the car, armed with several carrier bags and an extensive list.


'How did your presentation go at work today?'

'OK, but I had to implement my disaster recovery plan even before I started my presentation on business continuity.'

'Why? What on earth happened?'

'My fruit tart got smashed up during the train journey into work. By the time I arrived in the office it looked like a train wreck. I had to put it in the fridge to recover while I was doing my presentation.'

Mark smiled. He might have guessed there would be some drama associated with the number of cake tins Polly was determined to take into the office that morning. Anyone would have found it a challenge to carry that many tins and get them all there safely.

'That's the last time I'm baking for the office. I felt like crying when I saw the state of my tart. Bloody trains. Just my luck they cancelled mine and I had to cram in an overcrowded carriage. I even dropped the tin with my muffins in.'

'Were they OK?'

'Well, I think they probably bounced, they were disgusting and tasted like rubber. Don't think I'll be making them again.'

'What did the train wreck taste like?'

'Great. Provided you closed your eyes while eating it, I thought it was lovely. It all disappeared in a flash so I guess everyone agreed with me.'

'So, are you going to make one for the fete?'

'Definitely, and the carrot cake. Knowing that Edna will be judging this event there's no way I'm going to risk making the muffins. I would hate to give her the satisfaction of criticising my baking.'

'It's all done anonymously though. She won't know who made what,' Mark pointed out.

'That's true but I'd still hate to come last.'

# SIX

'Heard from Edna?' Lizzy had barely got through the door before asking Polly. She was desperate for a bit of gossip.

'No, why? Should I have?'

'According to the grapevine, she knows you're setting up a new club.' Lizzy seemed to hear most things on the grapevine. In fact, more often than not, she was the person starting the rumours.

Polly gloated at the thought of it.

'When you've finished,' Maggie interrupted Polly's *moment*, 'can we please get on with the meeting as I need to be somewhere afterwards.'

Polly called the meeting to order. 'OK. So, the hall is organised. Has anyone had any feedback from our posters?'

'One or two enquiries so it's looking promising.'

'Me too. The people who contacted me seemed quite excited at the prospect of a new daytime flower club.'

'Rose, are you OK to demonstrate?'

'S'pose so. Don't you want to do it?'

'I'll be recruiting and sorting out refreshments.'

Rose smiled. Already Polly was starting to sound a bit like Edna, but she thought it wiser not mention that to her.

'I'll have a think about what to do for the demonstration. Shall I get the flowers?'

'Yes, please.' Polly knew Rose wouldn't let her down. At least that was one less thing for Polly to remember.

'I think you only need to do two or three designs, something to whet the appetite.'

'Lizzy, can you help set up the hall with us?'

'No problem.'

'Sarah and I will get the refreshments laid out, then we're good to go. I just hope someone turns up.' Polly was concerned that this meeting might be a damp squib.

'So, we all know what we're doing then?'

There were general nods of approval and some chatting. 'Don't forget we've got an international designer doing a flower demonstration on Thursday in the town hall meeting rooms.

I'll be getting there early so I'll save you a seat,' promised Maggie.

'Brilliant. I'll probably be a few minutes late. It's a bit tight getting there from the office, especially if I get held up, however, I'll do my best. The rest of you, I'll see you at our new flower club on Saturday.' Polly beamed. Perhaps this new club would work after all.


Maggie arrived at the demonstration early as she had predicted and, knowing that Polly might be late, didn't want her to miss out on the wonderful cream cakes that were on offer as part of the ticket price. She put one of the chocolate eclairs on a plate and left it on the chair beside her for Polly.

Lizzy sat on the other side of her. The two of them were deep in conversation and didn't notice Edna's arrival. Edna recognised Maggie from the rear and noticed the vacant seat beside her. As the demonstration was just about to start, she quickly sat down, failing to see the chocolate eclair on the seat. She thought something felt strange but didn't want to make a fuss or disturb the demonstration.

Lizzy pulled a face at Maggie.

'What?' Maggie asked.

'Look who's beside you.'

Maggie turned her head and saw it was Edna. 'That's all we need,' she whispered to Lizzy. 'Polly will be furious when she arrives and sees her sitting there.'

'Never mind that,' laughed Lizzy, 'Edna's sitting on her cake.'

'No! Are you sure? Perhaps she moved it,' said Maggie, optimistically.

A few ladies nearby signalled for them to be quiet. The demonstrator was already well into creating her first flower arrangement. The door creaked open and Polly crept in. She spotted Maggie and then noticed Edna sitting next to her. The horror of that woman. She found a seat at the end of a row close to the stage.

The demonstration was fascinating, and Edna insisted upon turning to Maggie to speak to her, which made the situation even more awkward as she was in two minds whether or not to mention the cake. Surely Edna would have noticed had she sat down on it, she thought. She tried to glance inconspicuously around Edna's feet to see if she had put the plate on the floor, but her view was obstructed by Edna's huge handbag.

At the end of the demonstration Edna rushed towards the stage so she could be the first to take some photos of the designs. There was a gasp as she made her way to the stage. The eclair was well and truly stuck to Edna's bottom.

Polly looked over and Maggie headed towards her. 'Sorry about Edna nicking your seat and eclair,' she smirked. Polly couldn't control her laughter. 'This has made my day. That'll teach her, pinching my seat like that.'

Edna continued taking photos and then made her way to the car, totally oblivious that she was modelling an eclair. No one had the courage to say anything. It wasn't until she arrived home and went to get out of the car that she noticed the very squashed éclair on her seat. 'What the?' she exclaimed out loud. 'Where on earth has that come from?' George was waiting on the doorstep as he had seen Edna's car arrive.

'What's that, love?' he asked as he made his way to the car.

'Look,' Edna pointed to the eclair. George noticed the rather large stain on the back of Edna's skirt. 'It looks as though you might have put it there.' Edna twisted around to look at her skirt and realised that it must have been attached to her all afternoon.

Polly was still laughing when she got home. Mark looked up from his work. 'You seem happy. What's the joke?'

Polly showed Mark the photo she'd taken of Edna's skirt.

'Eurgh. What on earth's that?'

'That, is my chocolate eclair which Edna sat on.'

Mark looked puzzled. 'Why did she sit on your eclair? Did she know?'

'Doubt it.'

'Didn't you tell her?'

Polly pulled a face, as if *she* would tell Edna that she had a cake stuck on her bottom. 'No.'

'No one told her?'

'Don't think so.' Polly started laughing again. Mark wasn't sure what to make of the situation. 'In a way I feel sorry for Edna being the butt of your joke. No pun intended! How'd you feel if you were walking around with a cake stuck to your backside?' he asked.

'If you remember, I ended up wearing my chocolate brownie not that long ago, thanks to Edna. Therefore, I have zero, nada, absolutely no sympathy, especially as Maggie said the eclairs were delicious. I must phone Sarah and tell her.'

'You're awful,' laughed Mark as he headed to the kitchen to get a cup of tea.

# SEVEN

Freda had never been particularly outgoing. Her childhood was shaped very much by the strictness of her father. She was more like an invisible wallflower than a daughter. Her father made the rules about the house. *Absolutely no boys* was the number one rule. Freda had always thought of herself as rather plain and unattractive, or at least this is what her father told her. As a result, she would shy away from any possible interaction with men. Her parents had waited well into their mature years before having Freda, and the thought had crossed her mind that she either hadn't been planned, or she was born under sufferance of her mother to please her father. Her father was unable to hide his disappointment that she wasn't a boy and tended to withdraw from her. After her father had died, Freda still wasn't free of this suffocating relationship as, by then, her mother was ill and Freda looked after her for the next fifteen years of her life. Even though on a daily basis she thought that her mother was dying, or at least she said she was, she would make a miraculous recovery. She realised that her mother was lonely and didn't know how to cope on her own and that was why she insisted on Freda looking after her.

Living with her mother was a nightmare and extremely tiring. She didn't approve of anything Freda did. Whether it was her clothes, who she was meeting or why she needed to leave the house, it seemed that she couldn't do anything right. Friends and colleagues would tell Freda to leave, but she simply couldn't muster the courage to do this. Every time she so much as hinted that she may leave, her mother would produce an Oscar-worthy performance of a woman being abandoned and Freda decided it was easier to stay.

Years went by until finally the day came that her mother died, but instead of feeling a sense of relief Freda realised that perhaps she needed her mother more than she had imagined. Facing the big wide world on her own was a scary prospect. Apart from going out to work she didn't do much else. She remained in the same job for more than thirty years. Whilst she wasn't particularly happy there, it was all she'd ever known, and Freda failed to embrace change. New staff came and went and after all those years she was by far the oldest person there. As a result, she often got landed with the jobs no one else wanted to do or were capable of doing.

It was during this time when she was feeling somewhat low and sorry for herself, that she joined the local flower club. At least here she was with women of more or less similar age and with interests that appealed to her. As more years passed by, she felt content in her little world and lived happily with a rather bossy cat named Miss Tilly.

Despite not being particularly tech savvy, she decided to try and embrace modern technology. She started by investing in a mobile phone. Not that she wanted one that was top of the range, much to the disappointment of the salesman who was hoping to earn a hefty commission. Having spent the best part of an hour setting it up for her and explaining how to use it he was relieved he hadn't sold her a more complicated one. No amount of commission was worth having to go through all the phone's functions with Freda.

The next venture into modern technology was to buy a computer. 'Excuse me, young man, would you help me choose a computer?' The salesman looked about sixteen years of age to Freda, but as you get older, everyone appears younger to you. She noticed his name tag that read "Adam – how can I help you?".

'Yes of course I can,' replied Adam, not realising the full implications of his reply. Again, it was very challenging, more for the salesperson than Freda. He finally persuaded her to pay for it to be set up by their experts. At least that meant he could leave on time, otherwise he had visions of being stuck there all night with her.

The expert-man, Simon, explained the basic functions and suggested installing anti-virus software on the computer. All this sounded a bit too technical for Freda. She didn't know computers could catch viruses. She felt embarrassed to ask exactly what viruses they could catch but assumed that they were pretty deadly, the fact that it kept being mentioned. She was happy for the expert to take it to wherever they take them and set it all up for her.

'Do you use social media?' asked Simon. He could tell by the puzzled look on Freda's face that she didn't know what he was talking about. 'Look, I'll show you.' He opened up several screens of social media and Freda was impressed. 'What, you can talk to other people?'

'Absolutely. You can join groups, put photos up and make new friends. It's great. I've got five hundred friends now.' Freda was amazed.

'Five hundred! Do you really know that many people?'

'No of course I don't, but a lot are friends of friends, so you become friends on social media and you can see what everyone is getting up to.' Freda scanned through some of the posts people had put up.

'Why are there photos of people's dinners? Fancy putting that up for everyone to see.'

'You'd be amazed what people put out on social media. Just be careful, and if you're contacted out of the blue by someone you don't know, nor have any common friends with, be wary of them. There are some scam artists out there who try to befriend you and ask for money.'

'Really, that's shocking.' Freda couldn't quite get her head around this. Why anyone would try to become friends and get money from you wasn't something she'd come across before. She also found it hard to grasp the concept of speaking to people all round the world in a second. Simon set Freda's phone up with a social media account and email.

When Freda got home she couldn't wait to get online and put some photos of her beloved Miss Tilly on there for the world to see. Miss Tilly was the love of her life, although this cat had made it perfectly clear from day one that she would be the boss in this household. Freda, having been used to being the lowest in the pecking order, accepted her predicament without any protest.

Freda was excited to read various comments that had been posted about her photos. What lovely people, she thought. They all added photos of their own cats and dogs which Freda enjoyed seeing.

After posting a number of photos of Miss Tilly, Freda started to get friend requests. They were mainly from cat lover groups, but then a private message was posted from a young man in Morocco. This would be the start of Freda's infatuation with him. All of Simon's warnings were quickly forgotten. Mo was young and extremely good-looking. Not that his looks were important to Freda, but he came over as, what she would call, a beautiful soul. He looked after his mum and cared for his younger siblings. He seemed fascinated by everything Freda told him and in a matter of days the two of them were chatting online for several hours a day.

Freda was well and truly smitten with him. He said he was desperately saving for some new trainers, so Freda decided to treat him and forward the money to him.

'I'd love to meet you,' she announced one day.

'I'd love to meet you too, but I'm afraid everything I earn is spent on my family so there's no way I can afford to come to England. Plus, I would need to buy a visa and passport.'

Freda thought for a moment. 'I'll send you the money for the airline ticket and you can get your passport and visa sorted. It's no trouble.'

She really looked forward to being able to meet Mo in the flesh, although she wasn't too sure how it would end up because of the huge age difference and family circumstances, but she didn't want to throw away this opportunity of happiness.

'You are so kind, Freda. I am due to inherit some money soon from an uncle, so I'll pay you back as soon as possible.

I don't have a bank account, but my best friend has. If I send you his details, can you transfer it straight into that account rather than risk sending cash and I'll get the money from him.'

'Of course I can. Are you absolutely sure he'll give you the money?'

'We have been friends for all of our lives, so there is no problem there.'

Freda wasn't sure how to transfer the money, so she headed to her bank the following day.

'Are you sure you aren't being scammed?' asked a concerned bank teller.

'No, I'm not. I just want to know how to send money to him.'

'We need to set you up with online banking, then you can do that. We're just concerned about you sending such a large amount of money to this person without knowing him.'

'It's my money.'

'We appreciate that. It's just that there are a lot of scammers out there, so we always check with our customers before they send money, especially overseas.'

Freda couldn't imagine Mo doing that to her. As far as she was concerned, he wasn't far short of being a saint.

Having had her account set up online, and having the bank teller explaining what to do, Freda was able to transfer over the money as requested, and it wasn't long before she was transferring more money over so that Mo could buy a suitcase and clothes for his trip to the UK.

# EIGHT

Rose and Lizzy felt quite uncomfortable sitting around the table with Edna. She glared at them. She was desperate to ask them how Polly was getting on but didn't want to give them the satisfaction of her enquiring. She felt extremely disappointed that Rose and Lizzy were in the process of setting up another flower club with Polly. Clearly their loyalties lay elsewhere. It hadn't taken long for the grapevine to be spreading rumours about Polly's new club, even though it hadn't officially been launched yet, but a number of Edna's members had seen posters being displayed around the town.

Freda arrived, beaming. 'You look happy,' stated Edna, pleased to be able to take the tension out of the meeting.

'I've been chatting to a very nice young man on a website.'

Edna felt quite relieved that Freda had something to talk about and she could avoid having Lizzy gloating about the "eclair" incident. At the same time she was taken aback by what Freda had said. 'Really?'

'Yes. He's a fashion model and lives in Morocco. He's very caring and wants to know all about me. And he's going to come to England to meet me.' Freda was beside herself in excitement. 'Fancy that.'

'Sounds exciting,' Rose lied, concerned about her friend as alarm bells were ringing. 'How did you meet him?'

'It was all very exciting. I was just having a look at social media. I thought I'd better get with the times. I recently bought a phone and laptop. A very nice young sales assistant set up my accounts with access to social media sites so I could post pictures and share them with friends and family. It's all very interesting.'

Rose felt a pang of concern. Everyone knew that technology wasn't one of Freda's strong points and she suddenly felt worried about Freda's safety. 'And, how come you know him?'

'Well, that's a strange thing. He sent me a message saying he'd like to be my friend as he liked my profile.'

'Really?' asked Lizzy, not wanting to sound too patronising, but she knew that Freda didn't live a particularly exciting life at the best of times.

'He's just sorting out his passport and flight, then he'll come to the UK.'

'Did you say he's a model?'

'Yes, but he also works in the local shop and basically does any work he can as he looks after his mother and younger brother and sister. He's just lovely. What a wonderful person he is.'

'Then how is he going to be able to afford to come over here?' Rose's alarm bells were back.

'I've offered to book a flight for him as he's a bit short at the moment. All his money goes to help his mother, but he said he'd pay me back as soon as possible.'

'So, you've sent him money?' Although Edna wasn't savvy when it came to technology, nor dating, having been married to George pretty much all her adult life, she couldn't help thinking Freda was being taken for a ride.

Freda hesitated for a moment. 'Yes, some. I've sent him money for his ticket, and he also needed some to pay off a debt before leaving the country, but he's due to inherit some money soon, so he'll pay me back then. Apparently, a rich uncle has just died, so it's just a formality.'

Lizzy and Rose looked at each other.

'How much have you sent him?'

'About two thousand pounds so far. He's promised me he'll pay me back,' Freda repeated.

Edna looked worried. 'What do you know about him? Have you got a photo?'

Freda felt a bit put out. She had spent too many years alone and for someone to take an interest in her was exciting.

'I don't know why you're asking me all these questions. Can't you just be happy that I've found someone to love?'

'Of course, we are. We just want to make sure he is who he says he is and isn't taking you for a ride.'

Freda was feeling quite uncomfortable. At no point had she ever doubted him. 'Look, here he is.' Freda passed her phone around showing a photo of a very good-looking man, around 30 years her junior. 'That's Mo,' she said proudly. She could see the look of surprise on everyone's faces that she could attract such a lovely man.

'He looks really nice,' smiled Barbara who hadn't been taking much notice as she was still sorting out copies of minutes from the last meeting.

'Just be careful. Until you meet him you don't know if he's telling you the truth about anything,' Rose warned.

'OK, I get the picture,' said Freda, still feeling somewhat annoyed by everyone's reaction.

Lizzy could see Freda was embarrassed and changed the subject. 'What did you think of the flower dem the other day?'

Edna wasn't sure if she was asking out of interest or was rubbing it in with regard to the "eclair" incident. Judging by the look on Lizzy's face she was clearly aware of what had happened. 'I thought it was lovely. Shall we get on?' Edna tried to move the meeting on and not give Lizzy a chance to comment. This meeting was going to be hard enough for Edna as she was fully aware that anything she said would get back to Polly.

'We need to get new members from somewhere,' declared Edna.

'Youngsters don't really want to do flower arranging these days. They think it's for old ladies,' said Lizzy, well aware that Polly might struggle to get members too.

'What can we do to entice them?'

'Offer everyone free membership for a few months,' suggested Rose.

'We'd be bankrupt in no time if we did that.' Barbara was unimpressed. She found it difficult enough collecting subs from present members, let alone letting people attend meetings for free.

'Perhaps we should run more workshops.' Rose knew she was clutching at straws. Workshops were never very popular with the older members of the committee.

'We need to find someone famous who will take up flower arranging to make it popular again,' Lizzy piped up.

There was silence. Everyone was racking their brains trying to think of someone who would be interested in flower arranging. Edna looked at everyone. She was greeted with blank faces.

'OK, well, think about it but we must do something to attract more members. I've been looking at a few future events that might be worth us attending. There are various exhibitions coming up that could be useful. I think we should have a stand at them.'

Lizzy and Rose glanced at each other. They both kept quiet, hoping Edna wouldn't ask them to volunteer. They knew Polly was thinking of attending exhibitions too, and the last thing they wanted was a conflict of interest. Having had no response from anyone Edna moved the meeting on.

# NINE

'How many are you expecting to turn up?' enquired Mark. Polly looked up from piling cakes into the tins and boxes. 'No idea. Could be one, could be one hundred.'

Mark glanced at the line of containers on the table and laughed.

'Well, if only one turns up I hope they've got a big appetite.'

'I wanted to give everyone a choice.'

'Isn't this supposed to be a flower club and not a cake club?'

Polly ignored him and continued to carefully cut out the centre of her three-layer chocolate cake and fill it with chocolate buttons as a surprise, before putting the top layer of cake back and covering it with butter icing.

'Blimey. I think you might need a defibrillator on hand for anyone who has a slice of that one.'

Polly pulled a face. 'You won't be wanting any then, will you?'

He grinned. 'Just saying. Try and save a slice for me.'

Polly arrived at the dot of nine o'clock to make sure she had plenty of time to set the hall up perfectly. Any would-be flower arrangers were due to arrive at ten. Sarah was already in the car park and waiting to get stuck in.

'Give me a hand with all this stuff,' Polly called out to her.

Sarah looked in Polly's car at all the cake tins.

Polly pre-empted Sarah's comments.

'Yes, I know. I've baked loads of cakes.'

'Well at least everyone will have a choice.'

'That's exactly what I told Mark.'

They unloaded the car as quickly as possible and started setting up the tables.

'I think I'll sort out the refreshments and get the cake table set up.'

Sarah smiled.

'What?'

'You sound just like Edna.'

'Don't say that.'

'It's true. You and your cake table.'

Polly tried to ignore Sarah, although she did have a point. In no time Sarah had set up some tables and Polly had neatly arranged her cakes.

Rose arrived armed with buckets of flowers and proceeded to set them up on one of the rickety tables.

'I hope it doesn't collapse.' The tables had seen better days, as had the hall, but it was all they had so they had to make do. 'Shall I get started on making a few designs for people to see?' she asked, keen to get going.

'Good idea. If you can do that, once we've got a decent number of people here, I'll explain what we plan on doing with the flower club, then everyone can have a cup of tea and a slice of cake while they watch you do your dem. Is this OK?'

Rose nodded her approval and set to work with her various creations.

With more than ten minutes before the open morning was due to start a group of ladies appeared at the doorway.

'Are we in the right place for the flower club?' they asked.

'Absolutely. Come on in,' greeted Sarah, pleased that at least three people had arrived. The ladies walked into the hall, giving a sideways glance at the strange-looking heaters on the walls. 'Are they safe?' one asked.

'They're fine, just old,' Sarah reassured her, but wasn't feeling overly confident about them herself.

It was getting close to the start time and still only a few people were in the hall. Polly stood outside. People were walking by, clearly not interested in going to a flower demonstration. Polly decided to try a different tact. 'Come and join us for free coffee and cake and a flower demonstration.' It was starting to rain so people didn't need much persuasion.

Sarah and Rose looked at the doorway in disbelief as a never-ending crowd of people entered the hall. It was clear that most had come for free refreshments, plus it was now raining quite heavily outside, but there was always the chance they could be won over and take up flower arranging.

Polly nervously stood in front of the audience who were all seated and eagerly tucking into their free slices of cake.

'Welcome to our flower club. It's lovely to see so many people.' Polly suspected she wouldn't see many of them again. 'We are going to meet here monthly for a flower demonstration or workshop, and of course, a piece of cake.

Rose is going to do a short demonstration which I hope you will all enjoy. So, sit back and relax.'

Polly handed the microphone over to Rose. There wasn't much interest to begin with, the audience seemed more interested in the cake, but as Rose's flower arrangements began to take shape, she began to capture the audience's imagination.

To the sound of rapturous applause Rose ended her demonstration. Polly stood up.

'Thank you. From the applause it is clear you all enjoyed it. Going forward, there would be a nominal annual fee to join the flower club, and a donation towards refreshments, but we do hope you will consider joining us again. There're full details on the leaflets on your chairs. We hope you will come along next month.'

The audience gradually filtered out of the hall, not before one or two had grabbed a second piece of cake leaving just a few crumbs left on the plates.

'Well, that was a success, even if I say it myself,' Polly gloated.

'I think the proof is in the pudding.' Sarah brought her down to earth. Polly looked at her, a puzzled look on her face.

'Until next month we're not going to know how many are going to join. There's no way we'll ever see some of them again unless we just offer free coffee and cake.' Sarah had a point.

# TEN

Polly arrived at the church hall bright and early. She hadn't stepped into it since the incident at Edna's flower club a couple of months earlier, having decided not to attend the last meeting. So much has happened since then. After all, she now had her own flower club, albeit still in its infancy.

Gordon eagerly greeted her at the door.

'Polly, we're so thrilled you agreed to judge the exhibits this year. I'm sure you'll find them quite delightful.'

Polly stifled a snigger as she knew that Gordon had no idea what he was talking about. He wasn't much of an authority when it came to flower arranging.

'All the entries are in so you can begin judging whenever you're ready.'

'Thank you, will do,' Polly replied as she was directed in the direction of the flower arrangement exhibits.

'Just let me put my cakes down and I'll go and judge them.' Gordon nodded his approval as he noticed the baked items on the plate.

'They smell delicious,' he commented as he caught a waft of the cheese scones.

Polly made her way to the long bench table and placed down her various plates of baked goodies. There was no sign of Edna in the hall, although Polly was pretty sure she could hear her voice. She quickly headed in the direction of the flower competition just in case Edna appeared at the doorway.

Polly looked at the flower arrangements. It was quite a disappointing sight.

Class 1: "Gardener's Delight" featured just four arrangements; two of which were quite nice, and Polly suspected one of them might be Edna's as she recognised her style. She picked up her clipboard and started to judge the entries, awarding points for design, colour, plant material and overall interpretation. Two entries were, in Polly's eyes, quite laughable.

Edna had set up her flower arrangements before heading outside to talk to Gordon and other members of the show committee. She entered the room and without noticing Polly she headed straight for the baked goods competition. Since all the entries were in, she set about judging. All she was interested in was whether or not anyone had baked a cake as good as hers, although in her eyes no one could ever reach her standard.

She cut a small slice of one of the carrot cakes. It was quite dry. The second cake was slightly underbaked. She moved onto the third cake. It was quite delicious and melted in her mouth. That was definitely the winner as far as she was concerned. She was keen to turn over the exhibit card so she could see who had baked it but was being closely watched by one of the stewards who always accompanied the judges to make sure there was absolutely no cheating.

As Edna moved onto the fruit tarts she glanced over at the flower arranging class. She stopped what she was doing; a piece of fruit tart on a fork hovered in front of her mouth. She put it down and turned to one of the other judges who was engrossed in judging the runner beans.

'What's she doing here?'

'Polly's judging the flower arrangements this year. Our usual judge is on holiday, so we invited Polly to take on the task.'

Edna could feel her blood boiling and she sensed her face was turning red.

'Oh,' she replied, trying to quickly regain her composure. Had she known that Polly was going to judge the flower arrangements she would never have entered. Especially as one of the classes had only attracted two entries.

Polly was unaware of anything but the entries and fully engrossed in her task of judging.

She moved to Class 2: "Autumn Glow". There were just two arrangements in this class and neither excited Polly. She scrutinised the two designs. One had beautiful flowers, but the shape of the exhibit was all wrong. The other design had a beautiful shape, but Polly wasn't happy about some of the plant material especially as one or two accessories had been used. They seemed to be totally unnecessary and added little value to the design. Accessories were something Polly never approved of unless they were absolutely essential. She proceeded to place the relevant award cards by each design, although with only two exhibits to judge it was a difficult decision for her whether to place them first and second, or not bother with a first prize which she knew would be quite controversial and opt for second and third.

'It must be difficult when there's only a couple of entries,' commented the steward who was with Polly.

'It is. After all, this is a local show, not a national one and I don't want to put anyone off having a go at a future date, so I think I need to be kind.' With that she chose her favourite and awarded that the first prize.

As she moved onto the next class, she could sense that someone was staring at her. She looked across the room and saw Edna glaring. Polly smiled rather than ignoring her, knowing that would annoy Edna even more.

Edna tried to concentrate on the task in hand, but she couldn't stop herself from glancing in Polly's direction. Polly could feel Edna's eyes boring a hole in her back but continued with the judging.

As soon as Polly had finished, she headed out of the church hall.

Edna waited for her to leave then sidled up to the flower arrangements. She noticed that her Autumn Glow design had been given a second place and was furious. She picked up the award card and tried to swap it over with the card for the arrangement that had come first. Gordon spotted her and headed over to find out what she was doing.

'Finished judging the baked goods?' he asked, curious as to why she was standing there with a cheese scone in her hand.

Edna's cheeks flushed.

'I thought I'd have a look at the arrangements,' she stuttered, feeling very embarrassed. She was sure that Gordon must have sussed her out. He was well aware she had entered, as she did every year. She stopped what she was doing and hurriedly headed back to her station to finish the judging.

The baked goods competition always attracted a lot of entries and by the time Edna had finished judging it members of the public were already queuing up to come in, so she made a hasty retreat and didn't have time to see who the exhibitors were.

George was waiting for her outside. Her face was like thunder. He could tell immediately that Edna wasn't happy.

'I can't believe the nerve of that woman,' she said. George wasn't sure who she was talking about and was too afraid to ask. He looked blankly at her.

'Polly was judging the flower arrangements.'

'Isn't the judging done anonymously?'

'Well, yes, but I bet she cheated.'

'I don't see how she can, isn't it monitored?'

Edna ignored him.

'Let's go and have a look, rather than surmising,' suggested George, ever the peacemaker.

Edna approached the flower arrangement table to see the full results. To her horror she discovered the results were even more shocking than she could have imagined. She had been awarded a third prize for one of her exhibits, had won nothing for one of her designs and had come second out of two entries. She was furious. This meant that her points total was so low that for the first time in about ten years she had not won the coveted cup. She noticed Polly and Mark enter the hall and they were making a beeline straight for the baked goods.

Polly glanced down at the cards and was thrilled to see that her carrot cake had won her a first prize, as had her cheese scones and fruit tart. In fact, she had won a trophy for achieving the highest number of points in one category.

'Well done,' beamed Mark. 'I knew you would do it. How could anyone down-mark your baking? It's just the best.'

Polly glowed with pride. It wasn't that often that Mark praised her and it really meant a lot to her. She couldn't believe that Edna had awarded her such high marks.

She looked in the direction of the flower arrangements and noticed that Edna had a face like thunder. Edna stormed over to where she was standing.

'Well, I hope you're satisfied.' She spat out the words.

'I'm thrilled.' Polly thought she was talking about the baking competition.

'How dare you down-mark my exhibits,' she accused. Polly was taken completely by surprise.

'What do you mean?' asked Polly. She knew that Edna would have entered the various classes, but she had no real way of knowing which exhibit was hers.

'You deliberately down-marked me.'

'How could I? I didn't even know that you had entered,' Polly lied.

'Of course you knew. I always enter.'

Gordon, aware of voices being raised, moved swiftly across the hall to where Edna and Polly were having their stand-off.

'Ladies! Please!'

Edna ignored him.

'I'm really disappointed in you, Polly.'

'Whatever. You're only jealous.'

'Why would I ever be jealous of you,' Edna sneered.

'How dare you speak to me like that. I'm not one of your minions now.'

By then they had acquired an audience and most people in the room were looking over at the two women fighting.

'Ladies,' interrupted Gordon again. 'Can you both please calm down.' Edna stormed off in a huff.

'Sorry about that, Gordon. Edna disapproved of my judging.'

'Well, she is used to winning every year so this year I think it has come as a bit of a shock to her.'

'I chose the exhibits that I thought deserved the prizes. I had no idea that Edna had done any of them. How dare she accuse me of deliberately down-marking her work.'

'I'm sure you were fair. Please don't be upset by this. We really appreciated you coming along to judge them and hope that this situation hasn't put you off. We'd love to have you back next year. The other competitors really appreciated the helpful comments you put on their cards.'

Polly felt quite smug. Not only had she upset Edna, she'd managed to win over Gordon and let him see that she was the bigger person. Perhaps she would judge the show again next year after all.

# ELEVEN

'I think our meeting went well,' enthused Polly.

'Definitely. There was a lot of positive feedback.' Maggie and Rose were quite surprised that this idea of Polly's might actually work.

'Just have to hope they turn up next month,' insisted Sarah who still wasn't totally convinced.

'And pay for a membership,' chipped in Lizzy who was on the same wavelength as Sarah.

Polly ignored the negativity. 'So, what are we going to do next month?'

No one really knew. There was a lot of mumbling but no distinguishable ideas.

'Perhaps we just go to the wholesaler and see what's on offer.' Polly cut herself another rather generous slice of cake. Everyone stared at her. 'Are you enjoying that?' Maggie laughed.

'When have I ever not enjoyed a piece of cake? It helps me to think.' Polly tucked into the slice.

'Can I come with you? I need some flowers for the Scout fair that week. I've promised I'll demonstrate some flower arranging. Oh, and Polly, any chance you could bake some cakes?'

This was the last thing Polly needed right now as she was so busy. 'Suppose so,' she replied, although she wasn't feeling very enthusiastic about it. 'Let's have a committee meeting a day or two before our next club meeting to agree exactly what we're going to do.'

'I thought this *was* a committee meeting,' whined Maggie who didn't particularly like meetings at the best of times.

'This is a pre-meeting meeting,' Polly replied whilst trying to keep the crumbs in her mouth. 'It's an unofficial meeting over coffee. Our official meeting—'

'No doubt over coffee with cake,' interrupted Maggie.

'Of course.'

Maggie wasn't surprised that Polly had invented a new style of meeting as an excuse to have yet more cake.

'Tell everyone about the horticultural competition,' Sarah moved on.

'Oh yes, weren't you judging all the exhibits?' asked Rose.

'Well, as expected, there were hardly any exhibits to judge. Added to which, Edna entered all the classes. She was furious that I didn't award her first prize for any of her arrangements.'

Rose looked shocked. 'Oh no! Bet she was. Doesn't she usually win the cup?'

'Yes, but what could I do? Her arrangements weren't great.'

'Isn't it done anonymously?'

'It is, so there's no way she can complain. A steward accompanies all the judges so there's no way of identifying who has submitted each exhibit. It's only after awarding the prizes that you find out. But Edna had a tantrum and started shouting at me.'

'How did you get on with your baking?' Rose interrupted Polly's daydreaming.

'I won the cup!' boasted Polly. 'Edna judged the cakes as usual and gave me first place for every class I entered.'

Lizzy roared with laughter. 'No wonder Edna was so upset.'

'I'm dreading our next committee meeting. It was bad enough last time knowing that she had sat on the chocolate eclair.

Rose felt apprehensive about going. Lizzy, on the other hand, relished the thought.


For the second meeting in a row Edna wasn't looking forward to sitting around the table with Rose and Lizzy. She was sure that witch Polly would have told them what had happened at the horticultural show, or at least her side of the story.

Freda had phoned in sick, although Edna did wonder if she just wanted to avoid the meeting in case she was grilled again about her young man.

Rose and Lizzy sheepishly walked into the room and sat down, hoping to avoid any confrontation with Edna today, despite desperately wanting to gloat.

Edna had managed to get through nearly all of the meeting until Barbara piped up, 'How did the horticultural show go? Bet you won the cup again.' Edna flushed red.

'Er, not this year. It was nice for someone else to win,' she lied, trying to sound generous. Rose and Lizzy chose not to join the conversation as they had managed to get through this meeting quite quickly, with no confrontation and both had decided they'd like it to remain that way.

# TWELVE

izzy was not the greatest driver. In fact, Polly always offered to drive rather than accept a lift from her. Lizzy struggled to judge the size of her car and either left loads of room as if she was driving a bus, or she parked so closely to other cars that it was impossible to get the car door open. More often than not she ended up climbing into the passenger seat to exit her car.

Sarah and Polly were already parked outside the wholesalers and were waiting for Lizzy to arrive. 'There she is,' pointed Sarah as they saw her car turn into the car park. Lizzy spotted them and waved. Sarah was about to wave back but was stopped by Polly.

'Don't distract her.' Polly signalled to Lizzy that there was an empty space next to the motorbike area. Lizzy started to pull in but decided to manoeuvre backwards to make it easier for when she left. Next minute there was a scraping sound and the motorbikes fell over one by one.

'What the?' shouted a man nearby. 'What are you doing?'

He rushed over to his precious bike which was now on the ground with a broken headlight.

Lizzy panicked and tried to move her car, but the bike seemed to be attached to her side door and the more Lizzy moved the car the louder the scraping sound as the bike was dragged along.

By then a crowd was gathering.

'Oh, my god,' Sarah exclaimed. 'Better go and help.' By the time Polly and Sarah arrived at the carnage Lizzy was in tears and inconsolable.

'Do you want me to move the car?' offered Sarah who was a bit of an expert with parking.

Lizzy got out of the car and faced a couple of angry bikers, one of whom calmed down a bit when he saw the emotional state she was in.

'You alright, love?' he asked.

'I think so. She's just shaken,' interjected Polly. 'I'm sure all this can be sorted out. At least no one got hurt.'

'Yeah, but look at my bloody bike,' shouted another. 'Have you passed your test?' There was no calming this one. Lizzy was so distraught she couldn't answer. Sarah parked her car, pulled out her ever-present notebook and began taking down all the insurance details so that they could get on. Once all the paperwork had been done and numbers exchanged, Polly, Lizzy and Sarah entered the wholesaler.

Lizzy spotted a seat in the corner and decided to sit on it while Polly and Sarah looked around the fridge at the flowers.

'You OK?' asked Sarah, genuinely concerned about Lizzy who had by now turned a very pale shade.

'I'll be OK in a minute or two. I'm just a bit shaken.'

'Let's get on then.' Polly walked into the fridge area and wished she'd put on a cardigan. It was so cold there. She dashed out.

'Where are you going?' asked Sarah, wondering why Polly had done an about-turn. 'Back in a second,' she called over her shoulder as she headed for the ladies' toilet. She returned a few minutes later. 'That always happens when I come here.' She laughed. 'Now I can think straight.' Polly set about selecting various bunches of flowers.

She gathered up some roses which were on special offer. It was difficult to estimate how many flowers she needed as she couldn't predict how many would turn up on the day. She spotted reduced-price bunches of alstroemeria and carnations. She picked up as many as she could.

'Blimey, you're expecting a lot,' noted Lizzy.

'That's the problem. What if we don't have enough flowers? The last thing I want is for someone to go without.'

'Don't forget I need some flowers.'

'OK. Let's think this through logically. At the open day we had thirty people. Let's assume twenty of those turn up. What arrangement are they going to do?' asked Sarah, who was good at seeing situations objectively.

'Haven't decided yet. I suppose it depends on how many flowers I buy.'

'Well, how about we allow seven roses, a few stems of alstroemeria and a few stems of spray carnations each, that's a good starting point.'

Polly put back a few surplus bunches, along with some of the other flowers.

'We don't want to be left with loads of flowers. If more people turn up they'll just have to use more foliage.'

'Good thinking. I might just buy one spare bunch of each, to be on the safe side.' Sarah knew that Polly would worry if she didn't, so she let her pile them on the counter. Lizzy gathered up the few bunches of reduced flowers that Polly hadn't taken.

'How much? Are you sure that's correct?' Polly almost had heart failure after seeing the invoice.

The shop assistant double-checked it. ''fraid so. The VAT really adds up, doesn't it?'

'You're telling me. We'll just have to hope we get a good turnout.'

Lizzy dashed into Polly's house without knocking.

'You'll never guess what. My neighbour has been arrested.'

'Really? Why?' Polly was intrigued.

'Dunno, but I always thought there was something shady going on.' Lizzy rarely took anything at face value. To her there was always a more sinister side to everything, or at least she liked to think so.

'I thought you had quiet neighbours.'

'For most of the time but she has a few shady characters visiting. Also, I think she uses several names.

'Really?' Polly's ears pricked up. Perhaps Lizzy was right this time. Perhaps there was some scandal.

'Yes. I found a wallet on the path outside her house. I had a quick look inside and there was a credit card in her name, plus several others with different surnames and one for her daughter.'

'I thought her daughter was young?'

'She is. How would a twelve-year-old get a credit card?'

'I assume you gave them back to her.'

'Yes, of course. But I was standing for ages ringing the doorbell. It was obvious she was with a fella, and when she opened the door she seemed to be off her head on something.'

'Crikey. It all happens round your way, doesn't it?'

'Anyway, yesterday there was a real commotion, and the police took away a load of property. Late last night some shady bloke was standing in the front garden looking up at the house. I heard him saying that my neighbour had been arrested.'

'Blimey.' Polly noticed the time. 'Don't want to rush you but shouldn't you be on your way by now?'

'What time do you need to be at the Scout hall?' enquired Sarah.

'In half an hour's time. I'd better get going.' Lizzy picked up a bucket of flowers she'd bought at the wholesaler. Polly had added a few that she'd decided she wasn't going to use. She followed her to the car with the tins of cake.

'I'll need my tins back for tomorrow evening so I can use them for our club meeting. I hope these cakes raise loads of money for charity,' said Polly as Lizzy loaded them into her car.

'Thanks for doing this, Polly. I know the Scouts really appreciate it.'

'No problem. See you.' In a flash Lizzy had shot off down the road with the bucket of flowers in the front passenger footwell and the tins balanced precariously on her back seat.

Polly winced. 'I hope those cakes are going to be OK. If she brakes suddenly, they'll all end up on the floor.'

'Well, it's not your problem. It's up to her. After all, it's Lizzy's job to get them to the hall safely for their charity event.'

'True, let's get on with our meeting. So, what are we going to do at the workshop?' Polly opened the meeting.

They all assessed the variety of flowers in the buckets.

'How about a topiary,' suggested Maggie. 'They're easy enough.'

'Well, easy apart from the fact that I have to fix the sticks in with plaster of Paris. Last time I got into a real mess,' reminisced Polly.

Rose laughed. 'And the sticks weren't even straight.' Maggie remembered the sight of the leaning topiaries the group had made. Polly had been impatient waiting for the plaster to set and attempted to prop the sticks up with newspaper. That was a great idea until she accidentally knocked the table that the pots were sitting on. The slightest vibration had caused the sticks to slant, which was only noticeable when Polly removed the newspaper.

'We haven't got enough flowers for that anyway,' Sarah pointed out. 'What about a stacked arrangement?' They're great unless you need to make an emergency stop in the car on the way home as then the top arrangement goes flying.' Sarah recalled an incident she'd had after making one at a workshop. She had set off with her beautiful design safely on the back seat, but someone had cut in front of her. She applied her brakes a little too sharply. Half of her design was safely on the back seat. The other half ended up in the passenger footwell.

'How about a standard basket design. That's a pretty safe option,' suggested Polly.

'Safe, providing the basket doesn't leak and you end up with a puddle on your table,' pointed out Maggie.

'Let's keep it simple, then. I'll demonstrate a basket

design. We can get some cheap baskets either from a charity shop or pound shop and we can place a dish inside them just to be on the safe side. If we bring a lot of garden foliage to fill it out we should have enough flowers.'

'On a slightly different topic, I was wondering if it would be good to include children in the following month's meeting,' Rose broached the subject.

Polly's mouth dropped open. 'Children?'

'Yes. It's half-term and I just wondered if we could suggest that people bring their children and grandchildren.'

Sarah glanced over at Polly. Her views were pretty much on a par with Polly's with regard to children, but she wondered if Rose had a valid point.

'What do you think, Maggie?'

'Sounds like a good idea to me. After all, you're not inviting them to every meeting, but if it means people come, then it might work.'

'I just don't want us to become a creche for people to drop off their kids.' Polly wasn't totally convinced.

Sarah could see that Polly wasn't keen on the idea. 'Why don't we see how we get on at the next meeting. If it goes well, then invite them, but if no one turns up, then this isn't even an issue.'

Polly could always rely on Sarah to suggest something sensible. Whilst Polly wanted the meeting to be a success, now a part of her was hoping not many people would turn up.

Lizzy was so busy imagining what was going on with her neighbour that she hadn't noticed her speed as she approached the notorious bend by the Cow and Duck pub.

In a split second her car was skidding across the road as her wheels locked and she lost control. She held her breath as the car clipped the kerb and started to roll over.

A flood of water rained down on Lizzy's head, closely followed by the sound of cake tins being thrown around the car, firstly in one direction and then in the other as the car ended up on its roof.

Fortunately, there were a number of people enjoying a pint or two outside the Cow and Duck. They witnessed the whole event and rushed over to her aid. It wasn't long before the fire brigade had arrived on the scene and were attempting to right her car and retrieve a very wet Lizzy from the wreckage.

The doorbell rang. Polly got up to answer it. Standing on her doorstep was a slightly bemused firefighter.

'I think these must belong to you.' He passed Polly one of her cake tins, the contents of which were completely smashed up. Another of his colleagues followed suit, until Polly's hallway was full of smashed-up cakes.

'What's going on?' Sarah called from the living room.

'I'm afraid your friend has had an accident,' informed the firefighter.

'What, where?' By then Maggie and Rose had joined everyone in the hallway.

'Along the country lane by the Cow and Duck pub.'

'Oh, my god,' exclaimed Maggie. 'Is she OK?'

'She rolled the car onto its roof.'

Polly was frozen to the spot. 'Rolled the car?'

'We had to cut her out. She was taken to hospital purely as a precaution. She was quite shaken up by it all, but I don't think she sustained any serious injury apart from a few bruises. She's fine, so don't worry.' The firefighter tried to put Polly's mind at ease.

'Thank goodness for that.' Sarah was relieved.

'She won't be fine when I get my hands on her.' Polly laughed.

'I'm afraid the car's a write-off. Your friend said she was worried about getting the cakes tins back to you. I don't think she realised how battered they were.'

'Thank goodness these cakes were freebies. It would have been very embarrassing had they been for a paying customer.'

Polly was relieved but also felt rather annoyed. Lizzy just continued to amaze her with her driving skills, or lack thereof.

'Shame these cakes are smashed up, they look delicious.' The second firefighter was salivating.

'I'm sure they'd be perfectly edible if you closed your eyes,' laughed Polly. 'They were for a charity event. Hold on a second.' Polly rushed into the kitchen and bagged up some of the fruit scones that she had made that were still warm from the oven. 'Have these as a thank you. I appreciate you bringing my tins back,' she said as she handed them over.

'That's very kind of you.' He smiled, and off he went clutching the bag of baked goodies.

Polly and Sarah made their way to the kitchen with the tins of cakes.

'Is none of it salvageable?' asked Maggie who hated throwing anything away. Polly opened the tins and looked at the mess of crumbs and icing.

'You're welcome to it,' laughed Polly.

# THIRTEEN

Polly looked nervously at all the ladies who were waiting expectantly for her to begin the demonstration. She'd never demonstrated before and the thought of it gave her the collywobbles. Doubts crossed her mind and she thought fleetingly that she might not be able to do this. Sarah recognised the concern on Polly's face and signalled to her to start.

In front of her were around twenty ladies, all different ages and claiming they had come for the flower arranging, although deep down she wondered if they were really there for the cakes and tea.

'Ladies. It's nice to see so many people here today,' she began, trying not to sound too excited about the turnout. 'We've picked a lovely day to have this workshop, a little bit different from last month.' It was the first time in weeks that the sun had shone, and it was streaming into the hall in between the curtains.

'Can we close the curtains?' asked one of the ladies. It seemed a shame to shut the sun out, but the consensus was that they had to be drawn, putting the hall into a strange darkness.

'I'm going to demonstrate a simple basket design for you.'

She picked up one of the many dishes she had brought for the event and placed it inside one of the baskets, then put it on the turntable in front of her. 'First of all, we need to attach our floral foam inside the dish. You need a frog and a piece of fix.'

One or two of the ladies looked puzzled. 'What do you mean *frog*?' asked one lady who was brave enough to ask the question.

'It's a special piece of plastic that fixes into the dish to hold the wet floral foam in place,' explained Polly, not realising that some people new to flower arranging might not understand the terminology now commonplace to her.

Some might have thought she included wildlife in her arrangements. Occasionally wildlife did appear in her designs, purely by chance, normally in the shape of snails who were tucking into the foliage.

She proceeded with the design, placing pieces of foliage in order to get the shape she wanted before placing in a selection of brightly coloured flowers. 'I love bright flowers,' she stated the obvious. There were a few ahs from the audience.

'Isn't that lovely,' said one of the ladies, convinced she could never make anything as pretty as that herself.

'So, just to recap, you need a small amount of foliage to start with. Come and collect a container and basket and your flowers and foliage.' Polly was almost trampled to death as a rush of ladies headed to the front of the hall and were grabbing flowers by the armful. Almost immediately the buckets were empty and a few ladies were complaining that there weren't enough flowers for them. Polly looked around the room. She couldn't believe how greedy some of the ladies had been. 'Ladies, might I remind you that you only need seven roses, one stem of spray carnations and a stem of alstroemeria. Can you please put any spares back in the buckets so that everyone can have some?'

One or two ladies apologised and readily handed over any spares they had, others weren't so keen to do this and reluctantly handed them back after a lot of moaning.

'Don't forget to fix your floral foam into your containers, ladies.' Polly could already sense that a number of ladies hadn't listened to a word she had said. She was aware that a few were chatting or gazing at their phones whilst she did the demonstration and now she was witnessing the beautiful flowers being destroyed by them.

'Please don't cut your roses until you know what length they need to be,' she said loudly, above the noise. She was behind one lady who was determined to force a rose into the floral foam with such ferocity that it came out the other side. 'You only need to push around half an inch of the stem into the foam otherwise you'll never get the other flowers in.'

Polly glanced around the room. 'You don't need huge amounts of foliage,' she shouted, having been shocked that one lady was trying to cram a whole branch into her basket. So much so, that you couldn't even see the basket. Polly could sense she was about to lose her temper so she made a beeline for the kitchen where Sarah was sorting out refreshments, abandoning Rose to the chaos.

'What's up?' asked Sarah, somewhat surprised by Polly's sudden appearance.

'I'm counting to ten, otherwise I'm going to explode. No one has listened to a damn thing I've said.'

Sarah glanced into the hall. 'Everyone seems to be busy arranging flowers.' Rose was trying to get everyone back on track.

'It might appear like that but they're not cutting the stems properly and they're cramming the flowers in. Half haven't put foliage in yet. Others have whole trees sticking out. Doesn't anyone listen anymore?'

'Don't forget some of these ladies have never done anything like this before. It's all new to them.'

Polly sighed. 'Yes, but common sense and manners seem to have been left behind today.'

'Leave it with me,' reassured Sarah with her usual calm demeanour. 'You finish off making the tea, and I'll go and have a look to see if I can help at all.'

Polly continued sorting out the crockery and various cakes whilst Sarah headed into the hall. She returned a short time later laughing.

'See what you mean. It's not actually that bad, in fact some of the arrangements are starting to look really nice.'

'You're just saying that to cheer me up,' said Polly, not totally convinced. 'Give me a hand.' She passed a plate of cake slices to Sarah and followed her in with a tray of cups of tea.

Much to Polly's surprise, it appeared that Sarah was right. Several of the arrangements were definitely taking shape and didn't look bad for a first attempt. Perhaps Polly had set her sights too high initially and forgotten that everyone has to start somewhere.

Having finished their tea and cake the ladies started packing up. Polly walked around the room offering critique to the ladies over their designs. They all seemed very pleased with what they had produced. Polly felt quite euphoric.

'Thank you for coming today. I hope you've enjoyed yourselves and look forward to seeing you next month. We're inviting children to our next meeting as it's half-term, so if you want to bring your children or grandchildren along, please feel free to do so.' Polly couldn't believe she was inviting children. She'd never had any maternal instincts, and being around children wasn't something she felt comfortable with, but Rose and Maggie thought it would be a good idea and might encourage more members if they were child friendly.

'That seems to have been a success,' commented Lizzy who had arrived extremely late, now being reliant on public transport, and had missed Polly's near meltdown.

'Yes, it was,' replied Polly, pleased with the way events had unfolded and relieved that this, the first official flower club meeting, was over.

'Look at it as a learning curve. The more we run these classes, the better we'll be at it. If we manage to keep a good number of members, there's no reason why we can't turn this into something very successful.' Rose had a point, what came naturally to her didn't to other people so perhaps Polly had to be a little more patient in future. 'And don't forget that we've got kids coming next month.' Polly could feel herself going into a panic but having seen how this week's meeting had panned out, she wondered if perhaps Rose was right and that inviting children was a way forward.

Lizzy looked at her. 'Kids?'

'Yes, we decided it at our last committee meeting so we might encourage more people to attend.'

'Oh, sorry, I missed that.' Lizzy didn't want to remind herself of that evening when she ended up in hospital, so she headed into the kitchen to help wash up the cups and plates. 'How about we opt for disposable crockery in future? I don't like the idea of having to do this every time.' She wasn't impressed at having to put her newly manicured nails into a bowl of hot soapy water.

'Good idea,' said Sarah. 'Anything to make life easier.'

'And I'm going to sort out all the flowers and foliage into bunches to avoid the scrum next time.'

Lizzy looked bemused. 'Did I miss something?'

Polly forced a piece of chocolate into her mouth and closed her eyes. 'That's just what I needed. I think it's going to take me until next month to recover.' Lizzy was curious. She hated missing out on anything and knew that on this occasion she clearly had.

Sarah laughed. 'Nothing important, Lizzy. Some of the ladies were a bit pushy.'

'Understatement of the century,' laughed Polly.

'You look like you're in heaven eating that chocolate.' Polly snapped off another couple of squares.

'I am. This makes everything right.'

'How are your headaches these days?'

'I'm going to see an allergy therapist to try and get to the bottom of them.'

'What are you going to do if they say you can't eat chocolate ever again?' asked Lizzy innocently.

'That would finish her off totally,' chipped in Sarah.

Polly glared at Lizzy. She hadn't considered the possible results of an allergy test. The thought that chocolate might be the cause hadn't entered her mind.

# FOURTEEN

The phone call came completely out of the blue. Polly and Sarah were having a good old chat when the phone rang. 'Hello, Polly. It's Cynthia.' Polly hadn't heard from her for some time, not since she had suggested Polly set up her own flower club.

'How are things going?'

'Great, thanks. We've started the club and had a couple of meetings. So far, so good.'

'That's fabulous news. I'm actually phoning about the National Horticultural Show in London and wondered if you and Sarah would be interested in being part of the team. Polly was taken aback. 'We've just had confirmation that we can put in an exhibit. It's going to be a team event, and five people will form the team, along with the design team leader.'

'Who's that?'

'Elizabeth Dawson.'

'I don't know her,' Polly mouthed to Sarah. 'Hold on a second, Cynthia. Sarah's here with me now. Let me have a word.' Polly put her hand over the phone. 'Cynthia wondered if we'd like to be part of the team to do the big exhibit at the National Horticultural Show.'

'Us?' Sarah was surprised at being asked. 'I mean, yes. Let's.'

'That's a definite yes from the both of us,' Polly informed Cynthia.

'Wonderful news. I'll put you in touch with the team. I think they're having a preliminary meeting at the weekend if you can both make that. I know you've got a huge challenge ahead, but I'm sure you'll be able to pull this off and present something fabulous.'

'Wow. Us doing the National Horticultural Show.'

'I know. Not sure what to make of it. I wonder if they asked anyone else.' Sarah always doubted her ability.

'No. We were definitely top of the list,' insisted Polly, hoping that this was the case.


As Polly and Sarah pulled into a parking space outside Elizabeth's house, Polly's fears were about to be realised. A car swooped in front of them. Polly recognised it. 'Bloody hell.'

Sarah looked at the car. 'What?'

The passenger door opened and out got Amy. She glared in Sarah's direction.

'Oh no, of all the people to be here.' It was common knowledge that Polly and Amy didn't get on, in fact they had history. The slur Polly had made against Amy, accusing her of sabotaging her exhibit at a previous flower show, had been talked about freely in the flower arranging world.

Amy's husband, Malcolm, drove off, leaving her standing on the pavement.

'We can't let her ruin this for us,' insisted Sarah, knowing full well that Polly wasn't at all happy at the thought of working alongside her arch-enemy.

For a split second Amy felt quite vulnerable having seen Polly and Sarah.

They followed her into the house.

'Hello. I'm Polly and this is Sarah.'

'Hello. I'm Elizabeth, the design team leader. Do come in and make yourself comfortable.' Elizabeth was an elderly woman who reminded Polly a bit of Edna. She'd obviously been doing flower arranging for some time and clearly thought she was a bit special by the fact that she had given herself a job title. The other ladies in the room introduced themselves.

'Hello. I'm Chelsie with an "ie", not an "ea".' She was more or less Polly and Sarah's age, although the more Polly looked at her the more she was convinced she'd *had some work done*. She clearly had a trout pout. Then there was Fiona, who was a very quiet lady and spoke with a tiny mouselike voice. Of course, there was Amy who had managed to occupy the last comfortable-looking chair in the room. Polly and Sarah sat themselves down on two very upright wooden chairs.

'Hello, lovely to meet you all. Isn't this exciting?' Chelsie enthused.

'I hope you all like dogs. This is Pickles,' informed Elizabeth as a black dog bounded into the room. He dashed about sniffing everyone before standing in front of Elizabeth and barking. He was a real cross-breed. Perhaps a little terrier, retriever and who knows what else. Elizabeth gave him one of his biscuits which he rushed off to eat on the floor of the kitchen.

'Ladies. We've got a big challenge ahead. We need to create a display that has the wow factor.'

'How big is it?'

'We have a space of six metres by seven metres.'

'That's huge.'

'It really is, so we need to think big. I was thinking of creating a Victorian garden,' suggested Elizabeth before any ideas had even been discussed.

This suggestion was greeted with little enthusiasm from everyone. Elizabeth sensed that perhaps she was on a different wavelength from the others.

'Alternatively, we could do a design to represent a masterpiece.'

Polly looked puzzled. 'Like what?'

'I was thinking we could interpret a Van Gogh or Picasso painting,' she explained.

No one commented immediately, then a quiet voice broke through the silence.

'How exactly would we do that?' Fiona wasn't overly impressed. Elizabeth hadn't given the actual logistics much thought and didn't reply.

'Why don't we do something fun?' piped up Sarah, much to Polly's surprise. Sarah rarely spoke out in front of people she didn't know. Polly smiled. 'Like the funfair or circus,' Sarah continued.

'Oh, yes, let's.' Fiona was suddenly very enthusiastic.

'We could have moving parts. Perhaps something rotating like horses on a merry-go-round, only we could make the horses out of flowers,' suggested Chelsie.

'Or how about a Ferris wheel and all the seats etc. could be made from flowers.'

The volume of everyone talking at once started to annoy Elizabeth. She felt disappointed that her ideas hadn't been met with as much enthusiasm.

'Wouldn't it be easier to go with one of my ideas?'

'If we want something that's going to grab people's attention it needs to be big and bold, surely?' Polly was determined that she wasn't going to back down and kowtow to Elizabeth's dusty old ideas. 'This needs to stop people dead in their tracks. No one has ever done anything like this before.'

'Perhaps they haven't because it's too ambitious.' Elizabeth still had doubts but realised that she was going to be outnumbered. 'OK, if we go with this idea, exactly how are we going to make it?' she conceded.

'If we constructed horses from wire frames, then covered them in flowers, they could go round the outside. In the middle we could have a Ferris wheel.' Polly was well away with her designing already. Once she became excited about a design, there was no stopping her.

'I agree with Polly. It would be great to have something so dynamic,' chipped in Amy. This had to be a first, for them to agree on anything. 'Do we know of any companies who could make this for us?'

'I actually have a contact we could use. He's very good and can turn his hand to most things,' Elizabeth bragged, happy to be taking back control of the discussion.

'That would be great.' Fiona was pleased she didn't have to search for anyone who could build such an extravagant exhibit.

'If we have a moving Ferris wheel, do we need anything else that's moving?' asked Polly.

'I don't think we want too many things moving. Surely something static would be good. We could make horses and dot them around the Ferris wheel just to be symbolic of the merry-go-round.' Chelsie was totally sold on the idea.

'If we put the Ferris wheel on a base of around two metres to give it stability, about one metre high, that will give us plenty of room to have the horses around the base.' Sarah was busy writing down details.

'How big should the Ferris wheel be?'

'If it was three metres in diameter that would have an impact, but not be so huge that it totally dominates our exhibit. After all, it doesn't have to be in scale, just needs to give the impression that it is a Ferris wheel.'

'So, we have a plan. Excellent.' Elizabeth clapped her hands and looked pleased with herself. 'Let's have something to eat.' She left the room and returned a few minutes later with plates of sandwiches and cakes. Pickles followed her into the living room and proceeded to put his nose on the edge of the coffee table in the hope that some food would find its way into his mouth.

'Pickles, leave Polly alone.'

'I don't mind. I love dogs.'

'Yes, but you don't want him eating your sandwich.'

'No, that's true.' Polly took a bite of the sandwich. It was fish paste. She grimaced. She hadn't eaten fish paste since she was a child and she'd hated it then too. Sarah could see Polly wasn't impressed. Pickles was still sniffing round the plates, his eyebrows twitching, soft brown eyes pleading starvation, so Polly discretely handed him the sandwich. He sniffed it and walked away. Sarah laughed quietly. Not even the dog would eat it. Polly didn't like to leave it, so she wrapped it in her serviette and sneaked it into her handbag. Sarah, being a complicated eater, made her excuses and filled up on biscuits and the lettuce and tomato which Elizabeth had used as garnish.

'Lovely lunch,' smiled Fiona. Polly wasn't sure if she was being serious.

'What are we going to wear?' asked Chelsie who clearly put a lot of importance on her clothes. She was wearing a very up-to-date outfit that Sarah would have loved to have worn but doubted it would suit her. Polly knew she'd never fit into anything like that, but Chelsie had such an incredible figure, she looked amazing. *Bitch*, thought Polly.

'Something bright please. Something that stands out from the crowd,' suggested Polly.

'We can sort that out closer to the time. In the meantime, I'll forward these details to my friend so they can start thinking about how to build this.' Elizabeth had finally got on board with the idea. It could actually work.

Polly and Sarah hastily got into the car. 'Well, that's great,' said Sarah, sarcastically. 'We've got a team leader like Edna and your arch-enemy is working on the project.'

'Yes, not ideal. You're forgetting darling Chelsie with an "ie" and not "ea".'

Polly laughed. 'I thought it was too good to be true. Not sure how I can work with Amy though.'

'She was remarkably quiet today.'

'I was very impressed with your ideas about the Ferris wheel. That really shut Elizabeth up.'

'Not sure she was too happy with my suggestion.'

'At least she was outnumbered. Fancy wanting to do a painting or Victorian scene. Dear oh dear.' Polly laughed.

'Fancy Amy agreeing with us too.'

'That's got to be a first.'

'I think this design will be incredible.'

'Do you think we're being a bit ambitious?' Sarah was feeling very concerned after the meeting, although it was her suggestion in the first place.

'Know what you mean, but won't it be amazing if we pull this off?' Polly enthused.

Sarah wasn't so sure, but she was always considerably more cautious than Polly when it came to flower designs. Sarah didn't like surprises at the best of times and tended to stick to designs she felt comfortable with. Polly, on the other hand, was afraid of nothing with her designs. The more outrageous and precarious the better so Sarah wasn't too surprised by Polly's reaction.

She was very quiet on the way home from the meeting. Polly sensed the reason and tried to reassure her.

'It'll be fine. After all, if it doesn't work Elizabeth will have to take the blame as she's team leader.'

'Yeah, but we'll all look stupid. People will associate failure with us and we won't get asked to do anything again.'

'Don't worry about it. If it's a failure, I'll tell everyone it had nothing to do with us.' Polly wasn't going to take the fall for Elizabeth if it all went wrong.

# FIFTEEN

'How did it go?'

'What, the club meeting?' Polly was still thinking about the meeting with Elizabeth and the team.

Maggie looked confused. 'Er, yes.'

'It went well,' chipped in Rose. 'It was a bit chaotic but ended up being a success.' She looked at Polly and could see that Polly's mind was elsewhere.

'Sorry, I'm thinking about another meeting,' Polly confessed. 'Sarah and I are going to be making a huge exhibit at the National Horticultural Show,' she blurted.

'Wow, that's incredible.' Maggie was genuinely excited for them both.

'You'll never guess who's on the team.' Sarah was bursting to tell her.

'Amy.' Polly got in first with the answer. Sarah gave her a sideways glance.

'Oh my God.' Lizzy couldn't believe her ears. She wondered if there'd be any arguments between them. 'How did she react when she saw you?'

'Quite civilised actually. She even agreed with us over the design.'

'Wonders will never cease. Can we get on with the meeting?' asked Maggie.

Polly reluctantly returned to the scribbled notes in front of her.

'So, we've got a kids day at the next club meeting,' reminded Rose.

Polly and Sarah still hadn't got their heads around this and didn't relish the thought of a load of screaming kids. Neither had any of their own nor possessed any maternal instincts. Having been persuaded by Rose that it was a good idea, they thought they'd better go through with this. Much to their relief, Rose had agreed to run the event and attempt to keep the children occupied enough to prevent Polly from going home with a migraine.

'I thought we could make a chicken in a basket.'

'A what?'

'You heard. It's very easy and great fun. All we need are some floral foam spheres that we join with a kebab stick, then we put loads of yellow chrysanthemums in.'

'What about the eyes?'

'I buy eyes for stuffed toys. We make the mouth out of ribbon. Then we can use a doily and a bit of ribbon for a bonnet. Hold on a second.' Rose got her phone out. 'Got a photo somewhere.'

'Sounds like fun to me.' Sarah leaned across while Rose scrolled through her collection of photographs.

'Yes. It'll be good to put the fun back in flowers.'

'Not that we take them too seriously.'

'No, but sometimes we worry about our arrangements, and this will give everyone a chance to chill out.'

Rose handed Polly her phone with the photo of the chicken she had previously made.

She burst out laughing. 'It's fantastic. I love it.'

'Her,' pointed out Rose. 'It's a her as she's wearing a bonnet.'

'Excuse me,' Polly apologised. She passed the phone to Sarah and Lizzy.

'That's brilliant. Everyone will love making one of these.'

'So that's decided.'

'I can get the flowers and materials,' offered Rose. 'Lizzy, would you like to come and help buy them?'

'Er, no thanks. I'm still recovering from the last time I visited the wholesalers.' Polly laughed. It would take a while before Lizzy got over the recent incidents with her car.

'Sorted out your car insurance yet?' asked Sarah, quite innocently.

'Do not get me started,' Lizzy began to rant. 'They're still dealing with the motorbikes, and now I've written the car off, they're offering me such a small amount of compensation, I'm not sure I'll be able to afford another car. Plus, they said that if I remain with them my insurance premium is likely to double and my excess quadruple.'

'Oh, dear, that's awful, I can see why you're angry.'

'What's the point of having insurance if they don't want to give you a decent payout when you need it? As they say, you're only insured until you want to make a claim.'

Rose felt sorry for Lizzy's run of bad luck. Polly, on the other hand, wasn't surprised that the insurance company didn't think Lizzy was a good bet for the future. She must have cost them a fortune with her recent claims. She knew from her own experience how excesses seemed to increase dramatically if you made an insurance claim. She had managed to break her laptop once as she carried it down the stairs. She was also carrying a large armful of laundry ready to put in the washing machine and she balanced her laptop on top of the pile. Having slipped on an overhanging sheet, the laptop ended up flying down the stairs and crashed straight into the front door. Trying to get an insurance payout proved extremely difficult. Polly was accused of deliberately breaking her laptop. Obviously, the insurance company didn't know that Polly was a walking disaster.

Polly changed the subject. 'I'm going to make some fun cakes rather than the more grown-up cakes.' She was looking forward to being a bit more creative with her baking and cake decorating. Her mind was already ticking over as to what creation she could come up with.

'So, we're all ready for a week on Saturday then? Lizzy, are you still OK to help Polly and me at the fete on Sunday?'

'Fine,' Lizzy was quite looking forward to the event. At least the venue was walking distance from her house.

'Great. We'll see you there. Rose and Maggie, are you sure we can't persuade you to come?' They shook their heads. 'Sorry, not this time.' Rose had already planned her weekend.

'Garden's flooded,' Mark shouted.

'I don't believe it.' Polly followed him out of the house, having to jump over a giant puddle that had accumulated in front of her doorstep. The water was so deep that, despite her efforts, she managed to put one foot in the puddle. There had been a cloud burst a short time earlier and the rainwater struggled to get through the pipework into the drain.

By the time Polly arrived at work she looked like a drowned rat. Her feet were still wet and with an umbrella that seemed to spend more time inside out than the right way round, she looked a sight.

She picked up the phone to call out the emergency plumbing service. By the time she'd come off the phone a small puddle of water had accumulated on the desk from her dripping hair. Work was going to be busy today and Polly knew it was unlikely she'd be able to get time off to sort out the flood. She just had to hope the plumbers managed to find the cause before the water crept in under her front door.

The call eventually came from the plumber who was pleased to have informed her that they had dug up the garden to the side of the house and uncovered the soakaway. Polly listened carefully as they relayed the work to her, and struggled to get a word in.

'What do you mean you dug up my garden to the side of my house?' The plumber went silent. 'I don't have a garden to the side of my house. My house is mid-terrace.' There was no reply. 'Are you still there?'

'Er yes. Sorry, I thought your house was at the end. We've dug up your neighbour's garden.' Polly took a sharp breath. That was the last thing she wanted. Her neighbours were particularly precious about their garden.

'Have you put everything back where you found it?'

'Yes, we've made good. They'll never know we've been here.' Polly wasn't convinced but would have to take his word for it and face the music when she got home if the garden was a mess.

'What are you doing?' asked Mark. Polly was keeping a careful watch from behind the curtain.

'Just waiting for next door to arrive home to see their reaction.' She didn't have to wait very long as Helen and Andrew pulled their car on the drive. As Helen got out of the car, she took a closer look at the garden and headed to Polly's house.

'Hello,' said Helen.

'Hello. Everything OK?'

'Well, yes. Do you know who has dug up our garden?' Polly knew she had to come clean and explained that the plumber had dug up the wrong garden.

Helen laughed, much to Polly's surprise. 'I was going to weed that flower bed and they've done it for me.'

'That's lucky.' Polly felt relieved, she was in no mood for any confrontation. She was angry enough that the plumbers hadn't come up with a solution to the problem of their garden flooding every time there was a cloudburst.


Polly pulled into the car park, if you could call it that. It was a very muddy field, and someone had attempted to absorb some of the rainwater by putting down sawdust.

'What the hell have we let ourselves in for?' asked Sarah, concerned that her expensive new hairdo was going to be totally ruined.

'Let's wait a few minutes to see if the rain eases off.' Polly tried to be optimistic.

'Do you think they'll cancel the event?'

'Doubt it.' This annual event had been running for years and never been cancelled before regardless of the weather.

'Bet no one turns up.' It wasn't like Sarah to sound so negative. 'I know I wouldn't bother if I didn't need to.'

'They said that it is always sunny when they have a fete

here. Just our luck that the year we decide to have a stand, it's like this.'

'Just hope they've got our gazebo set up. Don't think I want to do that in this weather.' Polly had been promised it would be ready and waiting for them.

They sat silently, deep in thought as the rain started to ease and the windows of the car steamed up.

Polly wiped the condensation from the window, then opened the door.

'Look, there's a patch of blue sky. I think it's clearing up now,' she said, trying to cheer Sarah up and perhaps instil some enthusiasm.

They got out and started to unload the car. Polly went on ahead to establish which site was hers. As she approached the gazebo her mouth dropped open.

'Oh my God, look at that.' She pointed at the huge bulge of water hanging down from the top of the gazebo.

'We've got to get that out otherwise it'll collapse.' She found an empty space to put down the box of flower arrangements and went to examine the collected water.

Standing underneath it, she tried to lift it, but it was far too heavy. 'We need a broom, or stick.'

Polly returned a few minutes later with an old broom that had seen better days. She positioned herself to the side and began prodding the gazebo in the hope of releasing the water. Sarah stood underneath it to offer support and in a split second the water was released and came crashing down to the side. Unfortunately, there were chairs positioned there so the water bounced off those and it was Sarah who ended up soaked. She gave out a cry.

All Polly could do was to try not to laugh.

Sarah turned to face her. All her clothes were wet right through, and her brand-new hairstyle was now a collection of dripping rats' tails.

'Oh, Sarah, I'm sorry,' Polly tried to say with some sincerity.

'This bloody thing,' snapped Sarah, clearly not in the mood for seeing the funny side of it.

'Let's get this stuff set up, then we can go home and get dried off before the fete starts this afternoon.' Polly headed to the car.

'Polly?'

'What's up?'

'This lady says we are in her allocated space,' replied Sarah, curtly. She was on a very short fuse by now.

'No, it's ours. We are definitely E23.'

Sarah called over to the organiser, who checked the paperwork and discovered that she and Polly should have been C23.

'I knew you were on our site,' said the woman.

'There's no way we're moving. Not now we've sorted out these gazebos,' insisted Polly. 'I was told this was our plot, and we're staying.'

The woman glared at her. 'This is quite ridiculous. You need to move.'

'Over my dead body.' Sarah was in no mood for this. 'Let's get unloaded.'

Polly moved her car and parked it as close to the gazebo as she dared. She quickly unpacked the folding tables and got them in position, ignoring the angry woman who had now accepted defeat, somewhat ungraciously. Rather hurriedly they covered the tables with cloths which Polly had folded so badly before packing them that they were now a mass of creases. Sarah looked at them with disapproval.

'There's nothing we can do about this now.' Polly attempted to smooth out the creases with her hands. Sarah tutted and rolled her eyes. In all honesty she was far from caring. All she wanted to do was get home and change out of her wet clothes. They literally threw the flower arrangements on the table and got back into the car just it was starting to rain again.

Polly revved up the engine. The car didn't want to move initially. She looked out of the side window and noticed the rear wheel was embedded in wet mud. She revved the car again in order to release the car. It was a success, although it was a shame it wasn't the same for their stand. Mud had splattered out from under the wheel and showered the tablecloth and the sides of the gazebo.

Polly looked over at Sarah.

'Oops.'

Sarah burst out laughing. 'Well at least no one is going to notice the creased tablecloths now. Let's get the hell outta here.' Polly obliged and the car slid across the field to the main road.

Reluctantly, after freshening up, they returned to the fete. By then the heavens had fully opened and everywhere was awash with water. Polly, having learned from a lesson earlier, parked her car on what appeared to be a drier part of the field in the hope she wouldn't repeat the mud disaster.

They squelched their way to their stand. Lizzy was there, looking concerned. 'Look at the state of our stand,' she pointed at the mud splatter. 'Polly did that,' Sarah quickly interjected.

Lizzy smiled. 'I might have guessed.'

'Excuse me, it was my *car* that made this mess.'

'You were the one revving it,' insisted Sarah.

'Well, you think *we* have problems, Polly pointed across the show ground. What was supposed to be an arena for the dog show was more like a paddling pool.

'Welcome to our summer fete,' boomed an echo across the tannoy system.

Polly laughed. Apart from a few brave stallholders there were only a handful of members of the public. All of them were sheltering under an old tarpaulin that had been draped rather precariously over some wooden poles outside the makeshift café.

'The band will now play,' boomed the voice.

The band burst into song, albeit very distorted, and the tinny sound kept cutting out.

'Where are they?' asked Lizzy.

'Who?'

'The band.'

Polly and Sarah scanned the showground. A minibus was weaving between the stalls and Polly noticed they were sitting in the minibus playing their instruments.

'Now I've seen everything.'

'Look.' Sarah and Lizzy could see the bedraggled musicians crammed into the back of the minibus, door open, trombones and trumpets sticking out into the open.

'Oh, how hilarious,' laughed Lizzy. 'Well, at least they've got the right idea. Only a fool would be out in this weather.'

'I'm going to go and get us a hot cup of tea and we'll hang around for another hour, then we'll leave if the weather doesn't clear up.'

'Good idea,' they agreed.

Polly made her way across the muddy showground, wishing she'd worn a long pair of boots. Her ankle boots were clearly inadequate for this type of terrain. By the time she had arrived at the café she was soaked from head to toe. She carefully carried three plastic cups of tea back to Lizzy and Sarah and they were greatly diluted by the time she arrived.

Some of the stall holders were already packing up much to the annoyance of the fete organisers who were convinced that the weather would clear up and crowds would appear.

'So much for us making money and recruiting more members. I'm not surprised Maggie and Rose opted not to come.'

'Had I known it was going to be like this, I'd have given you a few quid and not come,' laughed Lizzy. Sarah nodded in agreement. 'Let's go home, I'm cold, wet and fed up.'

They packed up everything and quickly loaded it into Polly's car before the organiser could stop them.

# SIXTEEN

Polly was slumped in the armchair when Mark arrived home. He looked over at her. 'You alright?'

He could see by the redness in Polly's eyes that everything was not alright and that she'd been crying.

'What's the matter?' He sat down on the footstool in front of her. It wasn't like Polly to be upset like this. Normally she was quite upbeat.

'You know I went and had the allergy test done.'

'Yep.' Mark nodded.

'Well, it's bad news. In fact, it's worse than that.'

Mark's brain tried to fathom what on earth Polly could be talking about. She'd gone along to be tested to try and get to the bottom of why she often had headaches. Surely an allergy therapist wouldn't be able to diagnose something seriously wrong with her, like a tumour.

'And?' he dared to ask.

'I'm allergic to chocolate.'

Mark burst out laughing.

'That's what's been making you so ill? I thought you

were going to tell me that you only had six months to live, or something like that.'

'An allergy therapist wouldn't know that. You idiot. This is devastating. How on earth am I going to cope without any chocolate?' Polly was annoyed at Mark's reaction and failure to understand what this meant to her, a chocoholic.

'If it's gonna make you better then surely it's worth giving up.'

'I dunno how I'll survive three months without any. What am I going to do?'

'More to the point, how am I going to cope with you and your withdrawal symptoms?'

The doorbell interrupted their conversation and Mark got up and went to answer it.

'Hi, Mark. Is Polly around?'

Mark nodded. 'She's just had some devastating news.' Mark kept his voice respectfully low and tried not to smile.

Alarm filled Sarah's face. Mark burst out laughing. 'I'll let Polly tell you,' he teased, heading to the kitchen to put the kettle on.

Sarah went into the lounge and found Polly seated in the armchair. She looked at Polly; a question in her eyes.

'Ignore him. I've just been told that I've got a food intolerance to chocolate.'

Sarah laughed. 'Bloody hell. I thought it was something dreadful.'

Polly sighed. 'Not you as well. It is dreadful news. Neither of you seem to understand the implications of this. If I don't eat at least two bars of chocolate a day I can't function.'

Sarah was aware of Polly's addiction but had always viewed it as a bit of a joke. Sarah had the annoying habit of being able to eat just one piece of chocolate at a time. Polly could never understand how anyone could do this.

'Surely when you've had one piece you have to eat the whole bar?' she'd asked her on one occasion as she snapped off a small square to eat.

'Nope.'

'But I don't understand how anyone can do that. When I start a bar of chocolate, no matter how big it is I must finish it,' she had said, brushing off intrusive thoughts that perhaps it was why she was forever needing to go on a diet, and Sarah always remained a very trim size twelve.

Mark reappeared at the doorway with some mugs of tea and the cake tin. He put the tray down on the table and opened the tin. Inside was Polly's latest chocolate cake creation.

'Fancy a piece, Sarah?'

'Now that's just being cruel.' She laughed. 'Yes please.'

He cut a piece for Sarah. Polly grabbed the knife from him and sat drooling over the cake. 'Well, it'd be a shame to waste it, wouldn't it? I'll start my withdrawal once we've eaten it.' She cut herself a large slice, larger than she would normally cut.

Mark smiled. 'Don't come crying to me when you've got a migraine,' he said unsympathetically, having seen the size of the slice of cake on Polly's plate.

'I know you love chocolate, but there are plenty of other cakes you can make that don't contain it.' Sarah tried to console, but it became clear that this was not the day to try and make her see sense as she watched Polly take a giant bite from the slice of cake.

Polly had worked well into the night decorating the various flavoured cupcakes she'd made. Before her was a plate of cakes covered in more chocolates than you could imagine; pink butterflies with pink and white candy; cupcakes that were meant to resemble ladybirds and some that looked like sheep. By the time she got to bed she was exhausted, and the kitchen looked like a bomb had hit it. She had tried so many cake icings that evening that she was on a real sugar high and couldn't switch off. Her head was starting to pound.

'Can't sleep?' Mark asked the obvious question as Polly tossed and turned.

'God, I feel sick,' she confessed.

'That'll teach you. I've no sympathy.' He had warned Polly that she would regret having to taste everything, especially as she was supposed to be avoiding chocolate, but his words had clearly fallen on deaf ears.

'I just wanted to make sure everything was alright but now the very thought of those cakes makes me feel sick.'

'Try to think of something else.'

'Like what?'

'Oh, I don't know. How about counting sheep.'

'Trouble is every time I do that all I see are those damned cupcakes.'

'Well, think of something else. What about your next flower design? That'll take your mind off it.'

Mark's suggestion was anything but true. Thinking about the huge exhibit Polly and Sarah were involved in was enough to give anyone nightmares. The thought of another gravity-defying creation wasn't something Polly was looking forward to; the last time she did something like this it ended up in a heap on the floor with her buried beneath it.

She tossed and turned for most of the night before drifting into an uneasy sleep shortly before the alarm clock went off.

Rose had been given the unenviable task of estimating how many flowers she would need for the workshop. It was never easy as some stems contained more flowers than others, added to which, the shades of yellow seemed to vary from one shop to another so, what was supposed to be straightforward, turned into an entire day's work for her. She also needed to wire and glue pairs of toy eyes for the children to use on the day. She didn't want any of them near a hot glue gun. It was well into the evening when Rose had finally got everything ready and she could have some rest before the big day.

Unusually, Rose was the first to arrive. Polly was normally on time, but today she was running late. As she arrived Rose could see that Polly didn't look too well.

'You OK? You look dreadful.' Rose stated the obvious.

'I don't feel that great. I didn't get much sleep and I woke up with a splitting headache.' This was the type brought on by a sugar rush and despite several hours having passed since she sampled all the cakes, it was clear her sugar levels were still probably off the scale.

She opened the doors to the hall and headed straight to the kitchen with all the cakes while Rose busied herself with unloading her car.

Sarah and Lizzy arrived a short time later. 'What do you want us to do?'

'I need the tables in rows, but not too close together,' she ordered. Sarah and Lizzy started moving the tables from the corner of the room. Polly came out of the kitchen holding her head. 'Any chance you could do that a bit more quietly?' As they both looked at her, the rather dilapidated legs of the table they were holding crashed to the floor.

Sarah laughed. 'Oh dear. Had a late night?'

'Not exactly. This isn't alcohol induced.'

'You haven't been eating chocolate, have you?' Lizzy was puzzled.

'What's chocolate got to do with it?' Rose had not been privy to this previous discussion.

'Nothing. I'm just giving it a rest for a while.' Polly hoped this would satisfy her.

'I was right, wasn't I? You're allergic to it, aren't you?' Lizzy gloated.

'Not exactly. I've just been told not to eat it for twelve weeks.'

'Because she's allergic to it,' chipped in Sarah.

Much to Polly's disdain, Lizzy and Sarah fell about laughing.

'Anyway, that's not why I've got a headache. I was up half the night getting these cakes made.' Polly thought it best to omit the fact that she had sampled all the icings and toppings.

'Sorry to interrupt, ladies, but can we get on?' Rose asked in a slightly formal way. She wasn't in the mood for frivolity at this time.

It wasn't too long before the room was ready, and everything was set up. 'OK, Lizzy, please open the doors.'

A small queue had congregated outside the hall and in no time they were heading inside.

'Good morning, everyone.' Rose attempted to get some level of quietness so she could start.

A couple of ladies were still chatting, and one or two children were chasing each other around the hall. Perhaps Polly had been right about inviting children, she thought. What was supposed to be an enjoyable morning arranging flowers could turn into chaos. Rather than get all uptight, Polly and Sarah decided to hide in the kitchen until Rose had got the group under control.

'Can we start?' Rose raised her voice and banged a pair of scissors on the table. Finally, she caught everyone's attention and most people looked at her. One or two were still keen to check their phones for some strange reason. Rose decided to ignore this and get started.

'I'm going to demonstrate how to make a chicken in a basket, then you can have a go.' She set about putting the yellow chrysanthemum into the floral spheres that were securely fixed into a basket. 'As you can see, I'm cutting the flowers with a very short stem and putting them close so there are no gaps.' As she completed the design and attached the eyes and beak, then fitted the bonnet, everyone started to clap. Clearly her idea for this class had gone down well as the children excitedly settled down at the various tables, with their mums, and in a short time everyone was engrossed in making the chickens. Rose had taken on board Polly's comment after the previous meeting, and allocated everyone a bunch of flowers so there was not going to be another scrum.

'Look at this.' Sarah gestured to Polly to look into the hall. 'I don't believe it. How on earth did she manage to get them under control?' Sarah laughed.

Lizzy headed to the kitchen. 'Well, that was easy, wasn't it? Perhaps we should invite children to all our meetings.'

'Don't even joke about it.' Polly wasn't convinced this was the direction in which she wanted her new club to go. But as she looked into the room it appeared that everyone was clearly following Rose's instructions, and it wasn't long before a number of cute-looking chickens were adorning the tables.

'I think we should wait a while before putting the cakes out otherwise the children will start running around again.' Sarah was right. The last thing they wanted was a room full of children on a sugar rush. Once the atmosphere was calm, Rose signalled to Polly that it was time for tea and cakes. No sooner had Polly put the cakes on the table than a stampede of children almost flattened her. They were all pointing at the cakes, wanting to try the different ones. It was all Polly could do to stop the grubby little fingers being pushed into the various icings. Polly started cutting slices and serving the tea. It wasn't long before there was silence, everyone tucking into the cakes, followed by some of the children becoming hyperactive with all the sugar and additives.

'So much for it going according to plan,' mocked Polly. 'Look at those children. They're hyper.'

'I did wonder if that would be the case, judging by all the cakes you made.' Rose didn't like to tell Polly that she thought she'd made a big mistake making so many iced cakes, but her fears were being realised.

Two children, in particular, were chasing each other around the room. Their mothers were chatting and trying to ignore their behaviour until the noise was so great it was impossible to do this. 'Sebastian, come here,' called out Angela. Sebastian glanced over his shoulder but carried on. 'Luke,' called out Suzy. He ignored her as he seemed intent on catching Sebastian and rolling around the floor with him.

Rose watched them and smiled.

'I keep getting those two kids mixed up,' said Lizzy.

'I know. It's uncanny how alike they look.' Rose managed to break up the fight and took hold of Sebastian's hand.

'Thought I'd better return him to you, Angela.'

'Sorry he's getting up to mischief.' Angela was concerned as Sebastian could be pretty full on.

'Not really, they're just having fun, but I suspect he's probably on a sugar high.'

Luke came over and sat in the chair next to his mum.

'Are the boys related?'

'No. We'd never met before we started coming here,' insisted Suzy.

'Your children look so alike.'

'Yes, it's strange, isn't it?' Suzy had noticed the similarities.

'Plus, they both seem to have the same mischievous personalities. It's almost as though they could be brothers,' noted Angela.

'Well, they certainly seem to get on OK.'

After a while everyone headed to the door, all armed with their chickens, and a slice of cake wrapped up in a serviette.

Polly looked around, taking in the state of the room.

'Looks like a bomb has hit this place.'

There were serviettes and plant material all over the floor, with a trail of cake crumb and icing.

Lizzy started to sweep whilst Polly tried to salvage some of the cake that hadn't had children's fingers stuck in it. Several of the cakes which were left had had the sweets removed by the children. Others were half-eaten and seemed to have been put back by the kids in favour of the next cake.

'We'd better get a move on. The knitting circle will be here soon. Sarah wiped over the tabletops.

'Think I might leave them a plate of cakes.'

'That's very generous of you, Polly,' smiled Rose.

'Not really. If I look at these cakes anymore, I think I'll be sick. I just want to get them out of my sight.'

Sarah laughed. 'That's got to be a first.'

# SEVENTEEN

'So, let's just recap about our workshop.' Polly opened the meeting.

'I, for one, thought it went well,' insisted Rose who was pleased with the way the event had gone.

'Apart from the mess at the end.' Polly always had to find some fault.

'Well, yes, there is that.'

'Only to be expected with children.' Maggie supported Rose's appraisal of the situation.

'They all seemed to have a great time.' Even Lizzy was starting to come onboard. 'Those two little boys – you know, Suzy and Angela's kids. They were so naughty, getting up to mischief.'

'I'm sure they were the ones who took the chocolate mice off the tops of all the cupcakes. I found sticky fingerprints all over the place.' Polly had been upset to see a number of her cakes had been messed with.

'That's probably why they were both so hyper.' Maggie had

a point. 'Strange how alike they are though,' she pondered. 'Angela and Suzy had never met before.'

'Well, that's a success. If nothing else, our club is helping people get to know others. And it's nice to get some younger people to join.'

'OK, I get it. We can have another kids day later in the year. Perhaps once or twice a year. Not sure I can cope with more than that.' Polly could tell she was going to be outnumbered.

Rose laughed. 'I thought you and Sarah coped very well. Let's see if we can organise something for Christmas, then they can all have a go at making a table arrangement.'

That was several months away and there were still far too many other things to be concerned about before that.

'Right. Let's get started.' Polly scrutinised her list of scrawled notes.

'You're very organised,' commented Lizzy, indicating Polly's list.

'I'm taking a leaf out of Sarah's book.' Sarah smiled, whilst knowing that had this been her notebook the notes would be neat, tidy and impeccable. Polly's were pages of doodles and random written words.

'There's a craft fair coming up at the exhibition centre in London in a few weeks' time. There are some spare tables and I've been asked if we'd like one at a knock-down price.'

Everyone looked blankly.

'And?'

'I think we should have a stand there. It would be good to advertise ourselves.' Polly felt pleased with herself that she had come up with an idea for getting new members and was now thinking of the future and how to build the club.

'Hold on a second,' Sarah interrupted Polly's daydream. 'This isn't going to be like the fete we did the other week, is it?'

Polly knew that Sarah still hadn't got over that. 'Promise it won't be. This'll be indoors for starters.'

'Phew. I'd just like it noted in the minutes that I never, ever, ever want to do another outdoor fete.'

Maggie muttered to Rose. 'Sounds like we had a lucky escape.'

'Too true,' chipped in Lizzy who overheard this comment. 'We got absolutely soaked, covered in mud and to add insult to injury we had no one come to the fete. We struggled to even give our soggy flower arrangements away.'

'I can assure you all that next year I'll be busy that weekend. I'd rather stick ten pounds in the pot and stay away,' insisted Sarah.

'I'm guessing you probably don't want to discuss another show then, but this craft one sounds promising.'

'No way.'

'I think it'll be good for us.' Polly wasn't going to accept defeat.

'That sounds more promising.' Rose felt quite upbeat about it.

'It's a craft show so there should be lots of people there. I thought we could make some flower arrangements to draw in the crowd.'

'Crowds love watching demonstrations, especially if there's something free.'

'That's what I thought. I had an idea about making flowers and turning them into fridge magnets.'

No one commented.

'Don't you think that's a good idea?'

'How does that connect with us?'

'We could stick a label on them with our details.'

Polly pulled out a crocheted flower from her bag. 'Look.'

'Oh, I see what you mean.'

'I can't crochet.'

'Nor can I.'

'I could knit some.'

'That would be great.'

'I can't do that either, I'm afraid. OK if I make flowers from something else?'

Polly wasn't too sure what Sarah had in mind but was fairly certain that whatever it was it would be fine.

'Lizzy, what about you? Can you make some?' asked Rose.

'Not really. I can't imagine anyone wanting anything I make.'

At least she was honest. Polly was well aware of Lizzy's attempt at craft work in the past. Most times whatever she made was caked in glue and looked an absolute mess.

'No problem, Lizzy. I'm sure we'll make enough between the rest of us.'

'So, let's get this in the diary. It's the last Saturday of the month. Rose and Maggie, if you could meet us there, we can work in rotation, so the same person isn't on the stand all the time.'


'You look busy,' Mark commented as he came into the lounge and found Polly sitting on the floor, surrounded by lots of different coloured wool, most of which was in a huge tangle in the centre.

'I'm making flowers.'

'What for?' Mark looked puzzled.

'The craft show. I think it'll be a good gimmick if we make loads of fridge magnets to give away so we can promote our flower club.'

'Haven't you got enough to do without this?'

'Eh?' Polly wasn't listening. She'd finally found the end of a piece of wool and was attempting to untangle the mess. She inched out another piece of yarn before coming to a complete standstill. She tugged at it and realised there was no way she would ever be able to unknot the wool. She pursed her lips and threw it across the room. 'I think I'll buy some new wool.'

'Sounds like a good idea to me.' Mark could sense that Polly's patience was wearing thin.

'Hopefully everyone's making something to give away.'

'How many do you plan to make?'

'Ideally a couple of hundred.'

Mark gasped. 'Surely people who go to this craft fair will be from all around the country, rather than local.'

'Some might be local.' Polly realised that she hadn't thought this through. It hadn't occurred to her that this might be a possibility.

'You never know.'

Mark was secretly thinking that this was yet another hair-brained idea of Polly's.

By the time the day of the craft show arrived Polly had a large collection of flowery fridge magnets, some had been crocheted or knitted. As Sarah could do neither she had made some extremely pretty ones using felt and buttons.

Polly compared her work to the others. Polly's were somewhat mismatched, having used a variety of yarns of different weights. Some didn't even look like flowers. She was dismayed to see that her crocheted flowers looked a bit bedraggled compared to Maggie's beautifully knitted ones and Sarah's ornately decorated felt flowers. They had been her idea, not theirs.

'Ladies, I've decided we need to be proactive with our recruitment drive. There's an exhibition coming up and I think we ought to be represented there.'

Rose took the sheet of paper from Edna and noted the date. It sounded familiar to her. 'Sorry, Edna. I'm pretty sure I have something planned for that day.'

'Me too,' chipped in Lizzy.

'Oh, well that's not very good. Someone's got to help.' She glanced over at the rest of the committee. Barbara had her head down as she was busy minuting the meeting.

'Can I count on you?'

Barbara glanced up. 'Oh, yes.' Not too sure what she had agreed to, but over the years she had learned not to upset Edna.

Edna could tell it hadn't fully registered with her. 'You'll come and help me with our stand at the show. Yes?'

'Yes, of course.' She hated attending any show at the best of times. Crowds always seemed to make her panic, but she could tell Edna was getting desperate.

'I might ask Amy to see if she'd like to join us.'

Lizzy looked at her in disbelief.

'Amy?' Her voice had come out in an unintentional squeal, having been startled by the very mention of her name.

'Yes, Amy. I know Polly and Amy were enemies, but now that Polly isn't on our committee, I don't see why Amy can't join us. She's really keen to join our club.'

Rose gave Lizzy a sideways glance. Little did Edna know that Amy and Polly were both working on the big exhibit for the National Horticultural Show and had temporarily put their differences aside.

# EIGHTEEN

'I 'll ask Mark if he'll drive us there, after all it would be a lot easier if we didn't have to mess around trying to park.'

Mark wasn't overly excited about the prospect, but he might have guessed he'd end up getting roped into helping Polly and the rest of the committee get themselves set up with their flower table at the huge craft exhibition.

It wasn't quite as stressful as they had anticipated it would be despite the car being packed full to capacity, Sarah being wedged on the back seat with Lizzy between an assortment of twigs and other floral sundries.

Polly hogged the front seat as she always did as she couldn't face sitting in the back of the car, but her journey was no more comfortable.

'There's hardly anywhere for me to put my feet,' she groaned, her knees reaching her chin as she tried to gently squeeze her feet in between bags and boxes of yet more floral material.

'Still, it'll be worth it in the end,' insisted Sarah, as usual, attempting to put a positive spin on things.

Mark pulled into the loading bay without too much trouble and helped Sarah and the wedged Lizzy out of the car.

A security guard headed in their direction.

'Have you got a trolley we can use?' asked Sarah hopefully.

'No. And you can't leave that stuff here.'

'Well, if you haven't got a trolley we'll have to go back and forth several times to unload.' Polly was in no mood for a jobsworth at this time of day.

The security guard glared at them, hands on hips.

Mark started to lift up some of the boxes.

'You can't leave your car here.'

'I'll only be a minute. I need to help carry all this inside.'

'Well, be quick. Other cars need to unload.'

'What a bloody wonderful start to the bloody day,' muttered Mark under his breath.

Polly picked up as many items as she could carry and walked into the huge hall in search of her stand. It was at the far end of the hall. Sod's Law.

She dumped everything on the floor and headed back to the car to pick up the next load. She had to laugh as she passed Lizzy and Sarah both looking like pack-mules with all the bags.

As she was gathering up the next lot of 'stuff' another car pulled in beside Mark's. It was so close to where Polly was standing that she almost had her foot crushed.

'Oi! Look where you're going,' Polly shouted out. She was glared at by a familiar face.

Getting out of the car was Edna. With her was Amy.

Edna barely acknowledged her, but you could see from her expression that she wasn't thrilled at seeing Polly there.

She had hoped to have promoted her flower club and didn't realise she would be in competition with Polly.

'What's up?' asked Sarah as she saw a pained expression on Polly's face.

'You'll never guess who's here.'

Before Sarah could answer she heard Edna's voice barking out her orders. It was unusual for Amy to take orders from anyone as she was usually the one who *wore the trousers*, but on this occasion she did as she was told.

'Girls, behave yourselves.' Mark gave them a playful wagging finger. 'See you at five pm.'

'Oh, no. What the hell is she doing here?' asked Lizzy. 'Oh, bloody hell. She wanted me and Rose to help her with an exhibition. She must have meant this one.'

Polly shrugged her shoulders and inwardly smiled. 'Just our luck. Especially as it looks like their stand is the one opposite ours.'

'What a bummer, still we'll show them,' replied Lizzy.

Sarah continued setting out their stand. It did look very impressive with the array of crafted items, along with all the crocheted flowers that they were going to hand out to visitors.

Polly set about making a couple of flower arrangements to put on the stand whilst Lizzy set up all their brochures and meticulously sorted out the buckets of flowers and foliage. Before they could finish Rose and Maggie arrived.

'Right. Where do you want us?' Maggie interrupted.

'If you could stand just over there,' indicating the other side of the table, 'and give everyone who passes one of our leaflets and a free crocheted flower.'

Maggie and Rose took up position and were alarmed to find Edna staring back at them.

Rose smiled awkwardly. 'Don't think I'll be flavour of the month at our next committee meeting,' she said out of the corner of her mouth.

'Did you know she was coming here?' asked Polly.

'I had no idea it was this show she was talking about. She was harping on about a show of some sort but in all honesty, I wasn't paying much attention. I told her I was busy this weekend!'

Lizzy laughed. 'Now we're for it. Edna took a lot of satisfaction in saying she was going to ask Amy to help her.'

'Little does she know that Polly and Amy have a truce at the moment.'

Although Rose's loyalties were to Polly and her new flower club she had decided to remain on Edna's committee. 'If I leave, who is going to keep her in check,' she'd said. Polly thought it was a great idea as it meant she had a *spy in the enemy camp*.

A voice came over the tannoy to announce that the show was officially open, and it wasn't long before a surge of people appeared in the hall, all desperate to find a bargain or some new craft idea.

As soon as they reached Polly's stand, they were pounced on by Rose and Maggie.

'Are you interested in flower arranging?' they asked the bewildered passers-by.

'I've never really thought about it,' they replied honestly.

'Flower arranging has changed a lot over the years. It's very craft-oriented these days,' said Lizzy, pointing to the designs that Sarah was busy demonstrating.

Polly placed one of her arrangements on the table in front of the lady.

'That's beautiful,' the lady said. 'I had no idea flower arranging was like this.'

'Have one of our crochet flowers as a memento.'

'And a leaflet about our flower club,' Rose urged, before the lady could sneak away.

Sarah looked up from the design she was making to find a huge crowd was watching her. For a second, she felt quite intimidated, so she put her head down and concentrated on making the designs.

'Aren't they lovely,' smiled Rose.

'You make it look so easy.' A compliment from an elderly lady in a rather garish coat.

'They're not that hard. It's just about having the right materials.'

Polly looked around the stall. Everyone was engaged with visitors and inundated with enquiries. She couldn't make flower arrangements quickly enough to keep up with sales. Sarah was totally overwhelmed by the number of orders she was receiving and was struggling to keep up with the pace.

Sarah eventually sat back in a chair. She hadn't stopped for a second since she'd arrived and was desperate for a break.

'I've got to get a cuppa or something,' she said to Maggie. 'I'm exhausted.'

'You and Polly go off for a break, we can manage the stand while you're away.'

Polly and Sarah located their handbags that had been buried beneath the pile of their coats under one of the tables. They walked past Edna's stand deliberately not looking, but Polly noticed out of the corner of her eye that no one was there. This was a huge comparison to the hordes of people crowding around her stand, all desperate to learn something new and come away with a free crochet flower.

Other members of Edna's committee had arrived to help although they wondered why they were there since they clearly weren't needed.

'Fancy Rose and Lizzy being on Polly's stand,' Barbara commented to Edna. Edna glowered.

'If they think this is appropriate behaviour, they've got another thing coming. They both said they were busy this weekend.'

'Well, they are,' smiled Barbara, aware that Edna was furious about the situation.

Amy found the situation quite funny. She wondered for a second if Edna was using her to try and annoy Polly.

'Perhaps we should have thought of a gimmick like theirs,' offered Freda, unhelpfully.

Edna was unimpressed by the suggestion. 'Just try and look busy,' she said as she decided to head off for a cup of tea.

She found herself just a few feet away from Polly and Sarah in the queue for refreshments.

Sarah looked around and spotted her.

'Hello, Edna. How's it going?'

'Fine,' Edna lied.

'Can't believe how busy it is here,' Sarah said, innocently.

Edna was prickly lately and wondered if this was a dig at her, but really, she knew Sarah well enough that there was no malice in her comment.

'It is, isn't it?' replied Edna as politely as she could. 'It's the first time I've been to one of these craft shows. I wasn't too sure what to expect.'

'Neither was I. There are loads of things I'd like to buy, if only I had the time to make all these wonderful things.'

Polly turned to Sarah. 'Do you want a piece of cake with your tea?'

Sarah scrutinised the pre-packed cakes that looked like they had been mass produced probably weeks earlier and turned up her nose.

'I don't think I want to waste my calories on that.'

Edna smiled. 'There's nothing like a home-baked cake.'

'Absolutely not, Edna.' Sarah agreed.

'You'd have made a packet here if you had baked some cakes,' chipped in Polly, deciding to put her differences aside for a moment with Edna, having seen the standard of the catering.

Edna suddenly felt a bit more relaxed. 'Perhaps next year I should bake cakes rather than promote the flower club,' she admitted.

'To be honest with you, Edna, I'm a bit surprised they decided to book both of us, especially so close. It's probably all about money. We had no idea you were coming here too, otherwise we might have thought twice about booking the table. It was an expense we could have done without.'

Edna felt pleased that this hadn't been a conspiracy after all. 'You've obviously got this event sussed out, judging by the number of people coming to your stand.'

'I think it's because we're giving freebies away. Everyone likes something for nothing.'

Edna knew that Polly was right.

'At the end of the day, all we're doing is promoting flower arranging. It's not like we're in competition with one another,' said Sarah, trying to build a few bridges between Edna and Polly.

Edna felt quite relieved to hear Sarah's view on it. Perhaps her and Polly shouldn't be at loggerheads after all.

'Nice chatting to you. Best get back to the stand.'

'Quite honestly, I feel I've overdosed on my craft items,' confessed Sarah. 'I thought I was going to be sitting down and having a relaxing day, but it's turned into a conveyor belt, and I can't keep up with demand. Not sure I feel like making any more.'

When they got back to the stand Sarah was relieved to see that Maggie had taken her place and was busy producing the craft items at a rate of knots.

'Do you want to take over?' she asked Sarah.

Sarah shook her head. 'No, thanks!'

# NINETEEN

Now that the club was established it became clear that most of the ladies were happy to make pretty much anything. They viewed the morning as more of a social get-together.

Maggie was impressed with the arrangements the ladies had made today. She had shown them how to make a parallel arrangement with rows of flowers forming a very bright design. Polly had managed to get a large number of reduced-price flowers from the local supermarket the previous evening. Some of the flowers looked a bit sad, but the others, she hoped, would at least last a few days before they gave up the ghost.

Friendships were being made in the club, which Polly was really excited to see. A number of the ladies who attended clearly met one another outside of club meetings. It was clear that this club was achieving what it set out to do.

'Do you want a lift home, Suzy?' asked Angela.

'Not today, thanks. My husband's picking me up, then we're going to the new DIY shop,' replied Suzy.

'Sounds fun.' Angela rolled her eyes sarcastically.

'Ha ha. I know. Derek's got next week off work and I've been going on at him for years to redecorate the spare room. He's finally agreed to do it.'

Suzy put on her coat and picked up her flower arrangement. 'See you ladies next month,' she called as she headed outside. Derek was already parked in front of the hall. He got out of the car to help Suzy load her arrangement.

Angela wasn't far behind her. She stopped dead in her tracks and stared at Derek.

He looked at her like he'd seen a ghost. The colour had drained from his face, and he dropped Suzy's flower arrangement onto the road. One or two flowers snapped off at their heads, leaving just stalks in the design.

'Derek,' Suzy called out. 'Look what you've done.' She looked at his shocked face and then followed the direction of his stare. Suzy frowned, not sure why Derek should have reacted in the way that he had or why Angela was looking equally as shocked.

'That's Angela,' said Suzy. A hint of recognition filled his face. 'Do you know each other?'

Before Derek could answer Angela was upon him. 'Daniel, what's going on here? You said you were abroad this week. Why are you with Suzy?'

'I'm sorry, Angela. Why are you speaking to my husband that way, and why are you calling him Daniel?' There was silence for a second. 'And what do you mean he was meant to be abroad? Derek?'

Derek was silent. His face slowly regained its colour as he tried to decide what action to take.

'Daniel is my husband,' said Angela, confused.

Suzy looked at Derek. 'He can't be. Derek?'

Derek looked blankly at her.

'We've been married for years,' informed Angela.

'Not exactly. We're not married.' He coughed.

'We've been living together for the past fifteen years and have two children, so we are as good as married.'

'No, Angela. Derek and I are married. I've got the certificate to prove it.' Suzy looked at Derek expectantly. 'Derek?'

Derek jumped into the car and in a split second he had driven off, leaving Suzy and Angela at the side of the road, both of them totally dumbfounded.

Polly was still clearing the hall with Lizzy and hadn't witnessed all the goings-on. Needless to say, Lizzy had sniffed out some gossip and was eagerly observing from one of the windows in the hall.

'Quick, Polly,' called Lizzy. 'You've got to see this.' Polly rushed over to the window to see what was so important. 'You know we thought Suzy and Angela's kids looked alike?'

Polly nodded.

'That's cos they have one dad. He's only been having it away with both of them.'

'No. Are you sure?'

'Definitely. They've all come face to face.'

'Where's he now?'

'He's driven off and left the two of them behind.'

Suzy and Angela were both looking upset and angry.

'I can't believe it. I thought I knew him so well, when all the time he's been having an affair,' said Suzy.

'Not exactly an affair.' Angela defended their relationship. 'As far as I'm concerned, we're as good as married. We've got a life together. What on earth am I going to tell my kids?'

'Sorry to butt in, but are you both OK?' asked Polly, whilst being genuinely concerned she was also grabbing at the opportunity to be nosey.

'I think I need to sit down,' said Suzy who was feeling decidedly faint.

'Come back inside and I'll make you a cup of tea. You look like you've had a nasty shock,' suggested Lizzy.

'There's no rush to get out of the hall for a while yet.' Polly unpacked the teabags, what was left of the milk and put the kettle on.

Lizzy sidled up beside Polly.

'I'm shocked,' she whispered. 'How dreadful to discover your husband has led a double life.'

'Wonder how he got away with it for so long.'

Polly quickly made the tea and took it to Suzy and Angela. She wasn't sure whether to hover or get out of the way. Curiosity got the better of her.

'Do you mind if I carry on packing up?' she asked, although she was more or less packed up already, but this gave her an excuse to earwig in on the conversation.

'I'll help,' said Lizzy, desperate to hear more of the saga.

Mark appeared at the doorway. 'Ready to load up?' he called out to Polly. She gave him a warning look.

'What?' he mouthed to her a little too loudly. She turned her head to the side, signalling with her eyes for him to go into the kitchen in the hope he would follow her.

He wasn't sure what she was signalling so he remained standing. He moved over to pick up one of the boxes.

'I'll help you with that,' said Polly as she rushed to follow him outside.

'What's happening? Why are those two women sitting there crying and ranting?'

'They've just found out that they've got the same partner.'

'No.'

'That's not the worst of it. Both have been with him for around fifteen years, and both have kids with him.'

Mark stared at her in disbelief.

'So did he marry both of them?'

'No. Only one. He's not a bigamist, just a dirty rotter.'

Back in the hall, no matter how hard he tried he couldn't stop staring at Suzy and Angela.

Lizzy was still pretending to be busy so she could listen to the conversation. She was bursting to say something.

'So, what are you going to do?' she blurted out, avoiding the filthy look Polly shot at her.

Suzy and Angela were both surprised by Lizzy's directness.

'No idea. I'm still trying to get my head around how I can be married to a man I clearly knew nothing about, that my life with him has been a complete lie.'

'Me too,' agreed Angela.

'What does he do for a living?' asked Lizzy.

'He works for the Home Office. Hush-hush work. That sort of thing,' said Angela feeling quite proud.

Suzy started to smile. 'What a load of rubbish. He's a long-distance lorry driver.'

Angela looked shocked. 'So even that was a lie? How do I know what to believe?'

'I don't really want to get involved,' Lizzy butted in, 'but I've seen him coming out of that new red building in town. I work just across the road from there and have seen him several times. I often bump into him in the sandwich shop near there.'

'Who have I married?' questioned Suzy.

'Suppose I'd better go home and see if he's there. If he is, he won't be for long as I'm throwing him out.'

'Well, I hope he doesn't expect to come and live with me. I'm throwing all his stuff out too.'

'Perhaps you need to let the dust settle and then discuss it. After all, you both have kids. What about them?' reasoned Polly, who was feeling concerned about them.

Angela and Suzy thought for a second.

'Perhaps you're right. But he'd better have a damned good explanation as to why he's done this to both of us.'

'Agreed.'

'Would you like a lift home, Suzy?' offered Angela.

'Please, if it's not too much trouble.'

By the time Polly and Mark had finished packing up the car everyone else had left. Polly felt sad and angry for Suzy and Angela. She was worried what rumours Lizzy was going to spread about them both.

'Blimey. I thought this flower arranging lark was just a bunch of flowers. I had no idea there'd be all this scandal.'

'You could write a book about it. It's incredible what goes on in people's lives. Ours is pretty normal by comparison.'

'Normal is good. I can deal with that.'


Polly sat and gazed across the room.

'Penny for your thoughts.' Mark wasn't used to seeing Polly so quiet.

'Just thinking about Suzy and Angela. How dreadful that both of them thought they were married to Derek or Daniel.'

'Can't believe neither suspected anything. After all, he was always away, spending time with the other family.'

'What d'you think will happen?'

'If he's got any sense, he'll steer well clear for a while. Then when it quietens down, he'll likely have a chat with both of them.'

'Wonder if either will want him back.'

'Expect so.'

Polly frowned. 'Do you really think so?'

'Yes, why not?'

Polly gasped. 'Well, if it was me, I wouldn't have him back.'

'What, so if you discovered I was secretly living with someone else you wouldn't want me back even though I love you?'

Polly began to smile; she knew Mark too well. 'Don't believe you'd ever do anything like that. You're such a bad liar I would see right through it.'

Mark grinned. 'Yeah, but what if I did?'

'I'd have to think long and hard about it,' replied Polly with a serious look on her face. 'Suppose we could sort out some sort of rota.'

'See, I knew you'd have me back.' He grinned that huge smile of his. The one which always melted Polly's heart.

Polly burst out laughing. 'You nut. Of course, I would. I couldn't imagine being without you. After all, who'd want me? I bet Lizzy is spreading all sorts of gossip.'

'Quite possibly.'

'I've never known anyone who's as bad as her.'

The telephone rang. It was Sarah. 'You'll never guess,' Polly blurted out, not even taking a breath, 'Suzy and Angela are only living with the same man.'

Mark laughed. 'Well, it didn't take long for you to spread the gossip. So much for Lizzy being the culprit.'

Polly put her hand over her phone. 'Well, I've got to tell Sarah, haven't I?'

Mark knew this would be a very long conversation, so he made a quick exit.

'What would you do if you discovered Mark had another girlfriend?' Sarah was curious, although it was clear Polly and Mark were soulmates.

'Dunno. I can't imagine him doing that to me.'

'No, but just supposing he did. Then what? Especially if you had kids with him.'

'Put like that, I'd be heartbroken that he'd lived another life and furious at the same time, that our life was a lie.'

'But what if he said he loved you both and couldn't choose between you both.'

'Suppose it depends on who the other woman is.'

'What if it was a man?'

'I'd be very upset. If it was a woman, I could compete but there's no way I could compete with a man.'

'It's an interesting dilemma. But I can't imagine Mark ever cheating on you. It's clear he's besotted.'

Sarah was right and Polly knew that. She'd definitely found herself a good one there.

# TWENTY

Elizabeth had sent the instructions to her 'someone' so they could make the base and Ferris wheel. The construction of them was pretty much complete and ready for viewing. Meanwhile she had found an old warehouse that was going to be demolished, but the owner had agreed to let Elizabeth and the team use it for a few months in exchange for a modest fee.

Sarah had been busy planning the horses that would stand around the perimeter of their exhibit. A local blacksmith had done a fabulous job making wire frames for the horses. The bigger issue for her was how she was going to get them all in her car. She put the seats down and managed to get one horse on the passenger seat and the other four crammed in the back, two of which had their heads sticking out of the side windows.

Polly couldn't stop laughing when she saw Sarah's car pulling into her road. 'I'm sorry, Polly, I won't be able to take you to the warehouse. I can barely fit in the car.'

'Come and look at this, Mark.'

Mark rushed out to see what Polly was so excited about.

'You're joking,' he laughed. 'Oh my God. Who are your friends? Aren't you going to introduce them to us?'

Sarah laughed. 'I didn't think I'd fit them all in. This is the only way I could do it. I do hope I don't get stopped by the police.'

'You should be OK, but they are sticking out a bit. If you have to drive down any narrow roads, I can see them getting their heads stuck in the hedgerows. Shall I put a couple in Polly's car?'

'That's a good idea.'

Mark lowered the seats in Polly's car, having moved an armful of rubbish out. 'Don't throw any of that away.'

'It's a load of rubbish.'

'No, it's not. I want to keep it.'

'OK I'll put it in the garage, and you can go through it.' He managed to fit two of the horses in, which made life a lot easier for Sarah.

'There. That's better. Giddy up,' he called, galloping his way back to the house.

Sarah was relieved that Mark had been around to help with this. She had worried about the drive to the warehouse.

They set off in convoy to the warehouse to meet up with the rest of the team. This would be their base for the next few weeks as they mocked up their design.

Polly's heart sank as she walked into the warehouse. She wasn't sure what to expect but she fully understood why it was going to be demolished. So much for a warehouse, it was more a dilapidated hall that should have been reduced to rubble years ago. Light came through the various holes in the roof, and she didn't want to explore what was in the corners. Whatever it was, it looked like it had been dead for a while. There were traces of rat droppings which sent a shiver down her spine.

Elizabeth greeted her. She didn't look too pleased with the environment either, but it was the best she could do with such a small budget. 'It'll be fine,' she said, trying to convince everyone, including herself. 'It's only for a few months while we get the exhibit ready.'

'Going to be a long few months,' Polly muttered under her breath.

'I just hope we don't see any rats,' said Chelsie. 'They terrify me.'

'Oh nonsense. They're probably more afraid of you. I'll bring Pickles along. He'll scare any away.'

'Let's get unpacked and ready for the delivery of our stand next week.'

They carried the horses into the warehouse. 'Oh, wow. They look fabulous,' commented Chelsie. 'You've done a great job, Sarah.'

'Well, I didn't make them, but thanks anyway.'

Elizabeth struggled to say anything positive about the horses. She knew they looked great but didn't want to let Sarah take the credit for the design.

Once they had set up the horses, the team felt excited at the prospect of seeing the stand. 'It's starting to come together nicely,' observed Fiona. 'Can't wait to see the Ferris wheel.'

'Ladies, we'll all meet over at the carpenter's studio next weekend to view the base for our design. I look forward to seeing you all then.'

Polly wished she'd worn a different pair of boots. She had soon realised the reason why the imitation suede fashion boots were so cheap. They looked great but they let in water and today it hadn't stopped raining since she got up.

She assumed she'd be able to park her car close to the carpenter's workshop but was wrong. There was no parking there, so she'd had to return to the main road and park in a very expensive car park, one which only accepted telephone payments, and then walk back to the workshop. By the time she got there her feet were soaking wet, and she was feeling the cold.

'What's up?' asked Sarah, curious as to the way Polly was walking.

'These damn boots. My feet are soaked and I'm freezing. Can today get any worse?'

Sarah pulled a face and pointed in the direction of an extremely large wooden box.

Polly's face dropped as she entered the building. In front of her was some sort of monstrosity.

'What the hell is that?' she asked, not realising quite how loud and curt-sounding her voice was.

'Our stand.'

'That's not our stand. Our stand is two metres across and one metre high.'

'I was asked to make it two metres high and one across,' replied the carpenter.

Polly looked at Elizabeth.

'Yes, that's right.' There was a note of uncertainty in her voice.

'No, it isn't. It's completely wrong,' insisted Polly. 'How are we going to put our Ferris wheel on that?'

Elizabeth was in no mood to argue, nor admit that she might have relayed the measurements incorrectly.

'Well, this is what we've got and we're not changing it now. We'll have to make it work.'

'But our Ferris wheel will be so high it will barely fit into the marquee,' stressed Sarah, who was feeling overcome with panic.

Polly stood in silence, speechless. She was afraid that if she did try to articulate her feelings then she was likely to release a barrage of abuse.

The others in the group arrived and stood around the 'stand' not realising quite what it was supposed to be. They all looked at each other and Polly pulled a face. In the end she couldn't keep her opinion to herself.

'This is our stand,' she blurted out.

The others looked at her.

'But I thought…' began Tracey.

'The Ferris wheel base was lower?'

'Exactly. The Ferris wheel will be far too high and how is it going to balance on a base that's only one metre wide.'

'It is what it is. This is our stand and we're not changing it,' interrupted Elizabeth.

'But this throws out the entire design. It's a monstrosity,' Sarah said, having decided she must add her opinion.

'My feelings exactly,' chipped in Polly. 'We never said it would be this tall. It'll be unstable.'

'They were the measurements I was given,' insisted the carpenter, realising that he was in the middle of a heated discussion.

Elizabeth glared at them. 'Let's work out how we're going to design the rest of the exhibit. I'm sure a few adjustments can be made.'

Polly was really feeling the cold. The wet socks had pretty much frozen around her feet and she was shuffling from one foot to the other in an attempt to keep warm.

Everyone in the group was starting to get irritated, partly due to the cold and the fact that they were having to quickly redesign the rest of the exhibit around this base.

'Shall we go and get a hot drink?' suggested Fiona.

'Good idea,' replied Polly, desperate to sit down and take her wet boots off.

In a split second, before Elizabeth could object, the group were heading to the café next door, without her.

They hadn't even sat down before everyone was moaning. 'What's she thinking? There's no way this stand will work.'

'Coffee?' Polly called across to Sarah. 'Please, with a double vodka in it.' Polly smiled, Sarah rarely drank alcohol, but she knew how she was thinking, she could do with a stiff drink right now.

'Cake?' she asked, which was greeted with, 'You bet. I need something for my sanity.'

Polly chose a couple of cakes that looked appealing and headed over to the table where the other ladies were sitting. She removed her boots, putting her feet on top of them near the radiator in the hope that she might be able to get her socks dry and her feet thawed out.

'Well, that's that,' said Amy. 'This bloody Ferris wheel will be the death of us. It would be tricky enough balancing it on a one-metre-high base that Elizabeth was insisting on, but two metres high, and only one metre wide, the whole thing is likely to topple.' Polly and Sarah looked at her with wide-eyed astonishment. They'd never heard her swear before, in fact they weren't even sure she knew any swear words and were quite taken aback by her comment, even though they were in complete agreement.

'If it does, it's Elizabeth's fault.' Chelsie was clearly unimpressed too.

'Yes, but it's us that would be made to look foolish,' insisted Sarah.

'There's no way she's going to budge on this one. We're just going to have to figure out a way around it.'

Elizabeth came into the café which was a cue for everyone to stop talking. She collected her cup of coffee and made her way to the table.

'I think it's looking fabulous,' she enthused. No one spoke. 'So, what are we all going to wear?' she asked, not realising that this was another delicate subject.

'Something bright and colourful, hopefully,' chipped in Polly who was never one to shy away from an over-the-top outfit. Sarah didn't speak. She hated bright colours and felt more comfortable in pastel shades, but she was so upset and angry about the stand that she didn't feel much like contributing to this conversation.

'The trouble is that what suits one person, might not suit another.' Fiona had rarely contributed during the whole of the planning process but was clearly concerned.

'Then perhaps we choose a colour scheme, and everyone dresses in those colours, rather than in the same outfit.' It was Amy who made the conciliatory suggestion.

'I do like the idea of everyone wearing a dress,' insisted Elizabeth. We are ladies and ought to look like ladies.' She looked around the table and was greeted with negative expressions.

'Yes, but you like short sleeveless dresses. I don't want my shoulders to show.'

'And I don't want my boobs to stand out. I try to find styles that minimise them rather than highlight them.'

'I prefer long dresses or trousers to hide my legs.'

Elizabeth frowned. 'I'm sure we can find something we all like and agree on.'

'Well, so long as it isn't orange.'

'I like orange, but hate red.'

'I can't wear yellow, especially that awful mustard colour.'

'Oh, I love that. It really suits me.'

'It makes me want to throw up. I had a raincoat in that colour when I was little. I was sick down it one day and now I can't look at that colour or I feel sick again!'

Sarah sat back and listened knowingly. There was no way they would ever agree on the same outfit.


Rose and Lizzy felt nervous attending the committee meeting. They sat opposite Edna and waited for her to speak. They were half expecting Edna to have a go at them for not supporting her at the exhibition. 'Well, I wasn't too impressed by the craft exhibition. If we do another one we need a gimmick like Polly had. I wish you two ladies had told me you were going with Polly.'

'We honestly didn't know you were both talking about the same exhibition.'

'We could have saved ourselves a lot of money paying for the stand and perhaps could have joined forces.' Rose and Lizzy glanced at each other.

'To be honest,' interrupted Rose, 'although it seemed to be a success and paid for itself, I'm doubtful Polly will get any new members from it. All the people who came to talk to us seemed to be from other parts of the country.'

'That's the problem with doing any event in London.'

'I thought as much,' Edna confessed.

Edna hadn't considered becoming Polly's ally but at the end of the day they both were trying to achieve the same thing. Lizzy cringed at the thought of Polly working with Edna and hoped Edna would forget about this idea. 'That would be good,' she lied. 'But I'm not sure if Polly's going to do another event. I think she's pretty fed up with events now.'

# TWENTY-ONE

'I suppose the question is, do either of us want him back?' Angela gazed into space.

'Not really, but it's not fair on the children.'

'Exactly. It's not their fault they've got a cheating ratbag for a father.'

'Dirty rotter.'

'In all honesty, I'd like to tell him to take a running jump. Things haven't been great between us for a while. I never knew when he'd be around or when he'd be home, he always seemed preoccupied.'

'Same here. I even wondered if he was having an affair. Friday before last he missed Luke's sports day. It broke his heart not having his dad there. I'm assuming he was with you.'

'No. I was furious with him too as we were supposed to be going out that afternoon. He told me he'd take the day off, but he didn't turn up. No word, nothing. When he did return that evening, we had a blazing row. He claimed he'd forgotten, but I'd reminded him only that morning. All very odd.'

'Wonder where he was then. Perhaps he was getting his leg over with someone else.'

'No. Do you think so?'

'He wouldn't dare. Would he?'

Angela's brain was ticking over.

'He's been behaving very strangely just lately. I wonder what's going on.'

'Yes, I'd noticed that too.'

'He told me we had to cut back on spending and suggested that I go back to work.'

'Same here. What on earth is he playing at? Don't tell me he's supporting a third family.'

'Doesn't bear thinking about. Well, there's only one way to find out.'

Suzy looked puzzled. 'What? Ask him? We'd never get the truth. He's a coward.'

'I'll get him followed.'

'What, get a private investigator?'

'Why not? A friend has just started up a business. I'll have a word and see if they can shed any light on what he's up to.'

Derek looked nervous. His hand trembled slightly as he poured sugar in his coffee. One or two grains landed on the table.

'What have you got to say for yourself?'

'I'm sorry.'

Angela and Suzy sat facing him.

'Sorry isn't good enough. Why did you do this?'

Derek looked blank, trying to find the right words, words which might calm things down a bit. None would come to mind.

'I thought you loved me.' It was Suzy who interrupted the silence.

'I do.'

'Then why did you go off with Angela?' She patted Angela's hand. 'Sorry, Angela, I'm not having a go at you, I just want to get to the bottom of this.'

'No offence taken.'

'I don't know,' he stuttered.

'I thought our marriage was fine. We have two beautiful children.'

'I know, I know. I just met Angela and fell in love with her. It was never planned. It's just something that happened.'

'How can you love both of us?'

'I do. That's the point. I couldn't choose between you both. I love both of you and our wonderful children.'

'Didn't it cross your mind at any time that this was wrong? Stringing us both along. Lying to us.' Angela wasn't ready to accept his explanation.

'How do we know you've not done this to anyone else?' Suzy was tearful. She dare not think that this could even be a possibility.

Derek looked from her to Angela, a look of guilt on his face. 'Er, no, of course not. Why would you even suggest such a thing?' His tone was indignant.

'I'm struggling to believe anything you say right now. Our marriage has been a lie.'

Derek felt sad for a moment. The realisation of what he'd done and the pain he had caused Suzy and Angela was becoming apparent.

# TWENTY-TWO

Despite Elizabeth trying to find a suitable outfit for everyone she had admitted defeat and sent the team out shopping together to try and find something they would all agree on.

'There's no way I'll fit into that,' exclaimed Polly, poking her pudgy tummy.

'Go on, at least try it.'

Polly reluctantly put one arm into the jacket. It just about fit, but there was no way she'd get her other arm in.

'Let's get a bigger size,' suggested Sarah.

Polly tried again. It fitted more or less, or rather less than more.

'I can't move my arms. These sleeves are so tight.'

'How about going up a size?'

'This is already bigger than I would normally wear,' protested Polly, yet knowing full well that all her clothes were starting to feel a bit snug. She looked embarrassed but reluctantly agreed.

The new size slipped on beautifully but by then it was

so large the rest of it hung from Polly like a sack of old potatoes.

'It looks dreadful,' she exclaimed.

'But it fits over your shoulders now.'

'And the hips.' Sarah tried to make her feel better.

'Yeah, but what about the rest? It has no shape. I look even fatter than ever.'

'We can put a few darts in it. It'll be fine.'

*I'd like to put a few darts in you right now*, she thought.

'I'm gonna need more than a few darts to make this fine.' Polly was feeling quite depressed about it all. She had been so excited about getting one of these flowery jackets, especially as Sarah looked so good in hers, but the realisation that this shape and design just didn't suit her had to be acknowledged.

'What's up?' asked Mark. He could hear Polly mumbling to herself in the hallway.

'Look, what do you think?' Polly entered the room wearing the jacket.

Mark laughed.

Polly's bottom lip began to tremble and she could feel tears begin to fill her eyes.

'O-kay...' Mark hesitated, desperate not to say the wrong thing.

'It's awful, isn't it?'

'It's not *that* bad.' He paused, wanting to avoid putting his big size eleven in it. 'Just a suggestion, but why don't you get one that fits?'

'I tried. This was the only one I could get my arms and boobs in. The smaller sizes I could only get one arm and one boob in.'

Mark pretended to scratch his face and tried to stifle his amusement. He could see she was distressed.

'Can't you wear something else? If you don't feel comfortable—'

'All the team are wearing these,' Polly interrupted. 'I'd be the odd one out.'

'I don't know what to suggest.'

Polly took the jacket off and flung it across the room. 'Bloody jacket,' she shouted and burst into tears.

Mark tried to calm her down. 'It's only a jacket, darling.'

'You don't get it,' cried Polly.

'Yes, I do. I know you want to look nice. To me you always look smashing.'

'Well, maybe to you but that doesn't count. It's not how others see me. All they see is a cake-stuffed overweight pudding!'

Mark picked up the jacket and handed it to Polly. 'Try it on again.'

Polly did as he suggested.

Mark asked her to do a turn and he looked it over. 'Can't it be taken in?'

'That's what Sarah said. Well, maybe she's right, but I've no idea who could do it.'

'Hold on a sec.' Picking up his phone he dialled a colleague's number.

'Hi, Linda. I wonder if you can help me. Or at least I wondered if your mum could help Polly. She's got a jacket that needs altering. Is this something your mum could do?'

He paused for a second. 'That's great. Thanks. I'll get Polly to pop over. Just give me the address.'

He quickly scribbled down the details and hung up. He handed the piece of paper to Polly.

'Linda said that her mum can alter this for you. If you want to pop over to the house now her mum is there, and she can fit it.'

Polly took the paper. It was just a short drive away. She still wasn't totally convinced but felt relieved that this plan might work.

'Are you forgetting something?' Mark asked as Polly was about to grab her bag and head out of the door. Polly looked back at him as he tapped his cheek with his finger.

'Thanks.' She smiled, and planted a noisy peck on his cheek.


'I'm going to put on lunch for the team,' announced Elizabeth, unexpectedly.

'That sounds nice.'

'I'll cook us all a meal and we can relax before we set up our design. Perhaps it could be a few days before the show.'

For most of the team, this was the last thing they wanted. Tempers had been frayed over recent weeks, and their patience was wearing thin.

'Suppose it might be OK,' Polly had said to Sarah as they headed home after another long day in the warehouse.

'You never know, perhaps she does have a heart after all.'

'There's probably some ulterior motive.'

'You're such a cynic. It'll be nice just to chill out and unwind for a day before the big event.' Polly hoped Sarah was right, but then Sarah always did try to put a positive spin on everything.

# TWENTY-THREE

ngela and Suzy stared at each other across the table. Angela was nursing a brown envelope that she played with in her hands.

'Go on, open it.'

'Once we do, there's no turning back.'

'I know.'

Angela took a deep breath and ripped open the end of the envelope. She pulled out a few photographs and a cover letter.

Suzy spread the photos out on the table.

They showed Derek and another woman. Angela read the accompanying letter from the private eye that they had engaged to investigate Derek.

'Her name is Debbie Green. She lives about five miles from here. No children.'

'I just can't get my head around this.'

'Who even is this man? He's a complete stranger. I can't believe that after fifteen years I know absolutely nothing about him.'

'Me too. How on earth did he think he could get away with all this? It's bad enough he cheated with you, no offence, but with this other woman too.'

'I know. It's unbelievable.'

'How could he sit in front of us and not own up to this? It just shows he has absolutely no integrity.'

'He hasn't got much of anything. Bastard. Pardon my French.'

'Well, let's see what he has to say about this at our next meeting.'


The colour drained from Derek's face as Suzy placed the photos in front of him.

'Where did you get these? Have you been following me?' He dared to challenge them about it.

'That's irrelevant. Fact is you lied. You sat there, promising that there was no one else. Bare. Faced. Lies. Derek.'

'Who is this Debbie woman? Does she know about us?'

Derek shook his head.

'Well, she will know soon. I'm going to tell her.'

'Please don't.'

'Excuse me? You expect us to keep your lie going? You really are something.'

'Does she have children?' Angela wanted to make sure that she wasn't pregnant, which could complicate the situation even more.

'No.'

'Well, that's a blessing. How many more lives are you planning to ruin?'

Derek couldn't answer. He knew he'd been caught out and nothing he had to say would remedy the situation.

The last thing Debbie had expected was the sight of two determined-looking ladies on her doorstep. She asked, somewhat hesitantly, 'Can I help you?'

'I'm Angela, this is Suzy. It would appear we all have something in common. Can we come in?'

Debbie frowned. They had taken her completely by surprise and she was unsure what to make of it. She wondered if this was some sort of scam, but she was intrigued to know what they had to say.

'Suppose so. Are you going to tell me what this is all about?'

Angela and Suzy made their way into the lounge. Sitting on the mantlepiece was a photo of Debbie with Derek. Angela nudged Suzy's arm.

She pointed to the photo. 'We've come to talk to you about this man.'

'Who? David? Is he alright? What's he done? Is he, any trouble?'

'You could say that, yes. He's up to his neck in it.'

'I don't know what he's told you, but I know Derek and we've been married for fifteen years.'

'I know him as Daniel, and I've been with him for fifteen years too. We both have children with him.'

'There must be some mistake. David and I have been together for the last five years. He said he didn't want any children.'

'Oh, I bet he did.'

'I'm sorry, love, but he's been stringing you along like the both of us.'

'I don't believe it.' Debbie's complexion had visibly paled. Her hands were shaking as she picked up her phone and dialled Derek's number. He didn't pick up.

'I think you need a cup of tea.'

'I need something stronger than that.' Debbie got up from the armchair and headed for a cabinet that housed numerous bottles of alcohol. She poured herself a drink and necked it. Suzy and Angela glanced at each other as she poured herself another drink.

'Are you going to be alright?'

Debbie wasn't sure how she felt, apart from sick. A feeling she couldn't describe swept over her. She dialled Derek's number again. This time he picked up. 'David, there are two ladies here, claiming to be married to you.'

There was silence. 'Are you there? I want an explanation.'

He stuttered. 'I can explain.'

'Well, I hope you can.'

'I'll be home soon.'

Derek knew he would have to face Debbie at some stage so he might as well get it over with, but he didn't want to return until Angela and Suzy had left.

'I'll let you know after I've spoken to him, but if what you say is true, he's not living here anymore.'

'Well, we don't want him back. We wondered where he'd gone after we'd kicked him out.'

'When was that?'

'A couple of weeks ago, after we'd discovered he'd been living a double life.'

'He told me he had some time off work so he'd be around a lot more.'

'What's his job?' Angela was interested to find out what story Derek had given Debbie.

'He works on the oil rigs. He's away for several weeks at a time.'

'He told me he worked for the Home Office. Suzy here thought he was a long-distance lorry driver. Fact is he works in town as an admin manager for an insurance company.'

Angela could see that Debbie was struggling to take it all in and accept that her life for the past five years had been a big, fat lie.

'Shall we go?' Suzy nodded.

'Look, Debbie, if you want to talk or meet for a coffee, please give us a ring.' Angela handed her a piece of paper with her phone number scribbled on it.

Debbie whispered, simply, 'Okay.'


It had been bad enough when Derek had come face to face with Angela and Suzy. Adding Debbie to the mix meant he was a nervous wreck. He sat in his car outside her house for a considerable time until he had plucked up the courage to go in and face the music.

Debbie made her feelings known in no uncertain terms. She had already bagged up his belongings.

'What's this, sweetheart?' Derek pointed to the black sacks piled up in the hall.

'What do you think? It's all your stuff. I don't want it.'

'Can't we sort this out? I love you. I'll leave Suzy for you.'

'What about Angela? Will you leave her too? You've strung both of them along. And for years! How dare you tell me you didn't want children when all the time you've got kids with Angela and Suzy.'

Derek had known that Debbie was keen to have children, but he had managed to talk her round and use his charm on her. Debbie could feel herself tearing up. She didn't want him to see her vulnerable side.

'Just go, David,' she ordered as she opened the front door. He hesitated, so she picked up one of the black sacks and threw it out onto the path. Derek finally took the hint and picked up the other bags and headed to his car. He got in and drove away. The earlier conversation with Angela and Suzy going through his mind. *Bitch*, he thought when he realised Angela had kept her word and told Debbie.

Derek checked into a local B&B but knew that money was running low and he couldn't carry on like this for much longer. Something needed to be worked out. He had been summoned to a local café by Debbie and was alarmed when he arrived and saw Angela, Suzy and Debbie there. He glared at Debbie.

'As far as I'm concerned, I want nothing more to do with you. I'm just here to give moral support to my sisters.'

'This is how it's going to be. Take it or leave it.' Angela laid out the terms. 'You live with me Monday, Wednesday and Fridays. You live with Suzy Tuesday, Thursday, and Saturdays. Sundays we'll alternate.'

'Is that understood?'

'Do I get a choice in this?'

'No,' chorused Angela and Suzy.

Derek looked completely defeated. It hadn't occurred to him that it would end like this.

'Oh, and you'll be in the spare room. You're the one who decided to sow your oats elsewhere. If it weren't for the children I'd wash my hands of you, but this is not their fault,' stressed Suzy.

'One other thing. Money. I can't believe you've taken our savings to pay for Angela. Sorry, Angela. I'm not having a dig at you, but I've discovered Derek has withdrawn most of our savings. Money we saved together for our family's future.'

'I had no idea. Have you spent our savings too?'

Derek nodded. 'Sorry, I had to.'

'If you couldn't afford to support two families how on earth did you ever think you could get away with it? I thought you were gambling, or something like that.'

'I'm sorry. I couldn't afford to pay all the bills. One thing led to another. I was hoping to get a promotion at work which would have come with a hefty pay rise, but I didn't get it so I'm stuck on my meagre salary for now.'

'Well, perhaps you need to get another job.'

'I'm working all hours now.'

'They're looking for shelf stackers at the supermarket. I've heard the pay is quite good.'

'Well, that would completely destroy my reputation and any chances of promotion if someone from work saw me. Can't you get a job?'

'Don't even think of it. This is your mess. If I take on a job, I'll have to pay for childcare.'

'Unless we shared the load,' interrupted Suzy. 'We could both find part-time work and share the childcare.'

'What a great idea.' Derek's face lit up.

'We're not bloody doing this for you, you idiot. This is so the kids don't have to go without. Trust you to only think of yourself as usual.'

'I'm just saying that I think this is a great idea. That way the children won't have to go without anything as there'll be money coming into the house. Houses.'

'We'll try it out for a month and see how well it works out for us and the children.'

# TWENTY-FOUR

'What on earth?' Mark stared at Polly while she lay in bed.

'What?'

'You're bright orange.' He laughed. 'Look at the sheets.'

Polly pulled back the duvet and noticed the new crisp white sheet had patches of orange-brown colours. She leapt out of bed, startling the cat who had been sleeping at the end of the bed.

'Oh my God,' she yelled from the bathroom.

She quickly turned the shower on and jumped under it in an attempt to scrub off as much of the fake tan as she could. The water around her feet was turning brown as the surplus tan started to come off. She felt relieved for a second until she got out and saw herself in the mirror.

The tan was very uneven. Her face was still orange, but her legs and arms were pale with patches of red from the vigorous scrubbing. Then there was the dark staining on her knees, ankles and elbows where she had failed to exfoliate prior to having the tan applied.

She stood in front of Mark, holding up a badly stained towel.

'Look at me. Just look at the state of me.'

He couldn't stop laughing. 'I did wonder. You started to darken up as the evening went on.'

'I wasn't expecting to look like this. I look like a freak.'

'You just look as though you've been sunbathing, apart from your arms and legs that is.'

'How am I going to face everyone today? Looks like I've smeared Marmite all over myself.'


Polly arrived at the warehouse wearing trousers and a long-sleeved shirt. Sarah had to do a double take.

'You OK?'

'No, I'm not. Look at the state of me.' She pointed to her face.

'Nothing wrong with that. It looks like you've just been on holiday.' Sarah tried to be as diplomatic as she could although Polly did look a sight. 'What about the rest of you?'

'I'm orange and blotchy. I just wanted to have a bit of colour to try to make my outfit look a bit better. I'm raw where I've been scrubbing this damned tan. Now I've got white arms and legs.'

Sarah looked at Polly's arms as she rolled up her sleeves.

'If we get a couple of days of sunshine, I'm sure the tan will even out a bit.'

'What are the others going to say?'

'Fact is, we're behind with our exhibit, so I'd have thought that they'd be more focussed on that than you. Nothing personal.'

Sarah had a point. They were still waiting for the motor to arrive to turn their Ferris wheel.

'Nothing happened since the last meeting?'

Pickles walked into the barn, took a cursory glance at Polly and cocked his leg over the base of the exhibit.

'Oh, lovely.' Sarah was weary.

'What's with the dog pee on everything? And something has clearly been chewing at this dried fruit.' Polly pointed to the teeth marks on a dehydrated orange. She was interrupted by a scream from Chelsie and looked up to see an incredibly large rat running across the floor.

Pickles spotted it and chased after it, knocking over a table and various boxes of materials in the process.

'Pickles!' roared Elizabeth. He totally ignored her. He'd picked up the scent of the rat and was desperately clawing at a hole in the wall where the rat had made a hasty exit.

'Pickles!' Elizabeth admonished. He looked in her direction and, having got bored with chasing the rat, walked over to her in the hope of getting a treat.

'If you're naughty again I'll put you in the car,' Elizabeth scolded him. Realising she wasn't happy with him and there was no treat to be had he settled himself down on the makeshift bed that had been built for him in the corner of the room.

'Today is getting worse by the second,' stated Polly.

After several hours of working Polly finally felt they were making progress. 'What d'you think?'

Sarah had been nervous about the construction part but was now warming to the idea. 'I think it could look fabulous if it all comes together on the day.'

Elizabeth overheard their conversation. 'It *is* going to be fabulous. It's exactly what I'd envisaged. Just like my design.'

Polly felt peeved. Elizabeth's design had been thrown out a long time ago.

'That was a delicious meal, Elizabeth.' Sarah was still licking her lips. It was a lovely change for someone else to cook a meal as she lived alone. Added to which, she had so many different dietary requirements that it always made things complicated whenever she was invited out to dinner. Elizabeth somehow managed to get it right.

Polly hated to admit it, but she'd enjoyed herself too. The dessert was especially tasty, a lovely pineapple and passion fruit pavlova. She had come back for seconds, and had she not felt a bit embarrassed, she possibly could have managed a third helping. Reminding herself that she was trying to lose a few pounds so that she could fit into her newly altered jacket she battled with the urge, yet still felt a little deprived when Sarah picked up the serving dish.

'We'll do the washing-up. Come on, Polly.' Elizabeth didn't put up much resistance. If anything, she was relieved that someone had offered as she had managed to dirty every pan in her kitchen.

'Bloody Hell.' Polly was shocked by the amount of clearing up needed.

'Me and my big mouth,' laughed Sarah. 'Come on, it won't take long if we both muck in.'

In no time at all, the dishwasher was loaded, the pans were cleaned, although one or two were so badly burnt on the bottom that it took a lot of salt, lemon juice and elbow grease to remove all traces of the lunch. Polly wondered if they'd ever been that clean before.

Sarah turned around. The waste disposal was groaning. She carried on with what she was doing.

'Pass me the sponge. I just need to wipe over this surface.'

Sarah looked around but could not see it. The waste disposal continued to groan.

'Oh no.' Polly noticed a small piece of the sponge disappearing inside the giant mouth of the waste disposal.

Sarah rushed over to turn it off and pulled out what remained of the sponge. 'Oh dear.' She laughed.

'Everything all right, ladies?' boomed Elizabeth's voice from the lounge.

'Almost finished,' shouted Polly, quickly stuffing what was left of the sponge into her pocket.

'We're just looking for a cloth to wipe over the surface.'

'There's a brand-new sponge on the side for you to use.'

Pickles rushed out into the kitchen and started barking at the waste disposal. 'Pickles, stop that,' shouted Elizabeth.

'Sorry, we can't find the sponge,' lied Polly.

'If that dog has taken it he'll be the death of me. He's always stealing and shredding them.'

Elizabeth handed Polly a new sponge so she could finish the task and went to sit back down in the lounge.

Pickles approached Polly and nuzzled against her. He seemed to know that she had the sponge in her pocket, and he wanted it.

'Don't you dare,' Sarah challenged. She could read Polly's mind.

'Well, if we give Pickles the remaining piece of sponge Elizabeth will think he chewed it.'

Before Polly could finish what she was saying, Pickles had pulled the sponge from her pocket and rushed into the lounge with his trophy.

'You're a naughty boy,' shouted Elizabeth.

'Poor Pickles. You really are wicked, Polly,' giggled Sarah. 'Let's get out of here before Elizabeth realises we've broken her waste disposal.' They made their excuses and headed for home, laughing all the way.

'Sorry I'm late,' Elizabeth apologised. 'I've been at the vets all morning. After some of the sponge had disappeared Pickles wasn't at all well. I assumed he'd eaten it, so I took him to the vet.'

Sarah and Polly glanced at each other.

'When they X-rayed him, they couldn't find any sponge. No idea where that went but they did find a button. Polly, I think this belongs to you.'

Elizabeth held out her hand. In it was a large wooden button.

Polly looked confused. She glanced down at her knitted jacket. The bottom button was missing.

'I had no idea Pickles had taken it.'

Polly felt genuinely remorseful. She had noticed Pickles paying her jumper a lot of attention. The bottom button had been loose for some time, One of those little sewing jobs that kept being forgotten.

'I'm so sorry, Elizabeth. Is he going to be OK?'

'He'll be fine. I wish I could say the same for my bank balance.'

Polly wasn't sure if Elizabeth was suggesting she should contribute to the large vet bill.

'Vet bills are high,' chipped in Sarah, aware that Polly wasn't sure what to do or say.

'This damned dog will bankrupt me,' smiled Elizabeth, much to Polly's relief. 'He's always taking things that don't belong to him.'

Polly headed over to the horse she'd been working on. 'That was a close shave,' she whispered to Sarah in an aside.

'Yeah, I think we need to stay out of her way today.'

Elizabeth was walking around the warehouse inspecting the design. 'Ladies, we need to start getting everything packed up. I've marked the boxes to make it easier for us when we get to the showground.

Polly looked at the row of boxes and shook her head. The first label read, "items needed for set-up". The second label read, "ready-made materials". 'Well, that's about as clear as mud,' she muttered to herself.

Elizabeth was standing guard and watching her like a hawk.

'Is this netting classed as ready-made or natural fibres?'

'Is there a problem, Polly?'

'Just not sure which box to put this in.'

'Do you need it for set-up?'

'Yes.'

'Then it goes in the set-up box. It's not that complicated.'

'Er, OK.'

Polly returned to where Sarah was. 'She's in a right old mood with me. I can't help it if I don't understand her labels.' Just as Polly was finishing her sentence, she heard Elizabeth snapping at Amy, on more or less the same subject.

Pickles had been eyeing up a cloth that was hanging over the edge of the table. As soon as Elizabeth looked away, he grabbed the opportunity to take it. The cloth was considerably larger than he must have thought. He gave it a gentle tug to begin with, but as it didn't move, he gritted his teeth and yanked it onto the floor, bringing with it Elizabeth's mug of coffee and several other items. 'Pickles! You naughty dog. Come back here immediately,' she screamed. Pickles, totally ignoring her, ran around the room dragging the cloth behind him until it got caught under the base of the exhibit. By then he had lost interest and headed back to the area of the warehouse where his basket was. 'You'll be the death of me,' shouted Elizabeth, her voice teetering on the edge of hysteria. 'Are we nearly finished, ladies? If so, I think we should call it a day and I'll see you all at the showground next week.'

Amy and Chelsie were surprised by Elizabeth's abrupt announcement as they still had some work to do but, neither of them being brave enough to challenge her, packed up their belongings and headed out to their cars.

'Wait, we're coming too,' shouted Sarah who was just as keen to leave. As she caught up with the others, she murmured, 'Let's hope she's in a better mood at set-up.'

# TWENTY-FIVE

'How are you two getting on with your big design?' Lizzy was wondering how Polly and Amy were working together and hoping for a bit of juicy gossip.

'OK I suppose.'

'You don't sound very sure of it.'

'Well, there was a difference of opinion. Plus, we had to traipse to a warehouse that's rat-infested.'

'Added to which, Pickles knocked over our exhibit while he was chasing a rat.'

'You what? I thought the team was all female.'

'It is. Pickles is Elizabeth's dog.'

'Oh, I see.'

'So, it's all been a bit of a challenge, has it?'

'Definitely. Elizabeth has a strange view of what clothes we're going to wear. We finally agreed on an outfit, but mine was a terrible fit. Luckily Mark knew someone who could alter it for me.'

'I'm sure you'll look great.'

'Providing it doesn't make me look fat.'

'Doubt it.'

'More cakes, anyone?'

Lizzy pondered. If Polly cut out a slice or two of cake she might fit into her outfit. Fortunately, for once, her internal sensor was working, and she didn't voice this opinion out loud.

Polly handed her the plate filled with a wonderful selection of her home-baked cakes.

'Don't mind if I do.'


'Today's the day.' Polly beamed.

'How d'you feel?'

'Excited. Scared. My stomach is churning but I can't wait to get there.'

Mark looked at the pile of things Polly had stacked by the front door.

'What's all this stuff?'

'I'm taking all that with me.'

'You'll never carry it all.'

'Yes, I will. I've dug out that wheeled trolley. I'm taking that.'

Mark laughed. 'That old bag-lady bag.'

'No, it's not. Everyone has them now.'

'I'm not so sure about that. My gran used to own one. She was always tripping people up with it,' he reminisced. 'We called it her ankle cracker.'

Polly had thought it a great idea to help get her flowers and "stuff" from A to B.

She started packing it as the doorbell rang.

Mark opened the door and laughed. In front of him was Sarah with her shopping trolley.

'What's so funny?' she asked innocently.

'Ignore him. He's being rude about our shopping trolleys.'

'I love mine. I don't care what I look like.'

'Or who you trip up,' quipped Mark.

All fully loaded, Polly and Sarah set off down the road towards the station with their shopping trolleys.

Mark stood on the step, totally bemused whilst watching them negotiate the pavement and other pedestrians with their trolleys.

'Bye. Good luck, girls.' He waved.

Shaking his head, he closed the door.


Polly's heart sank as she arrived at the station. Clearly there was a problem with the trains today as the platforms were heaving.

'Just our luck,' she commented to Sarah as they attempted to get their trolleys down the flight of stairs and onto the platform.

There were a few raised eyebrows and displays of annoyance as Polly and Sarah manoeuvred their trolleys past everyone.

The first train arrived and the people on the platform surged towards it.

'There's no way we'll get on that train. It's already so crowded,' Sarah despaired.

More and more people forced their way into the packed carriages and the doors struggled to close around them. After a couple of failed attempts, the doors finally closed and the train pulled away.

The number of people on the platform had reduced quite considerably, so Polly and Sarah edged forward. The next train arrived. It was still quite full, but Polly could see one or two gaps.

'What d'you think?'

Sarah looked into the carriage. 'Let's just risk it and try and get on, otherwise we could be here all day.'

They lifted their trolleys onto the train and pushed past a number of commuters who were standing by the door. Travelling during commute time probably wasn't the best decision they had made, but in order to get to the showground on time they had little choice.

Commuters weren't very patient with two laden shopping trolleys in their way and made their feelings known. Much to Polly and Sarah's relief the train was a fast one directly into London, so they didn't have too long to travel. As soon as they left the station, they hailed a waiting taxi that took them to the showground.

Polly could hardly contain her excitement as she entered the huge marquee for the show.

'I'd never imagined it to be this big.'

'Me neither. Now we've just got to find Elizabeth.'

They took in the interior of the marquee and marvelled at all the exhibitors setting up the produce that had taken weeks, if not months, to perfect. Vegetables the like of which Polly had never laid eyes upon before, to the stands of exotic orchids and insect-eating plants.

'Wow. Isn't it just incredible? I can hardly take it all in.'

Elizabeth had spotted them and was frantically waving to gain their attention.

'There she is. She's looking a bit stressed, isn't she?'

Polly had no idea what the next few days would bring. Elizabeth had marked out their pitch and already put the stand in position.

'It looks incredible,' oozed Chelsie, impressed that Elizabeth had been able to organise such a major project.

Amy was already there, rummaging through the various boxes of sundries.

'Could I have everyone's attention?' Elizabeth clapped her hands. 'Where is Fiona?'

'I'm sure she'll be here any minute.'

'Well, we can't wait around for her, let's get started. So, today is all about getting the mechanics right. Then tomorrow we put the flowers in.'

'I can't wait'. Polly was itching to get started.

'Dare I ask the question? Does the Ferris wheel work OK?'

'There are a few issues but I'm sure we can sort it out over the next couple of days. We won't concern ourselves with that yet.'

Sarah didn't agree. She'd feel considerably more relaxed if she knew the main component would work.

Polly could sense her concern. 'Let's get on and cover these horses to get them ready for our flowers.'

'OK.' Sarah reluctantly got stuck in and by the end of the day she was feeling more optimistic. The exhibit was taking shape nicely.

'It's going to look fantastic,' enthused Polly. 'Don't you think?'

'Yes, I agree, but I'd still like to know if the Ferris wheel will work. The ground is very uneven here.'

'Don't worry about it. I'm sure we'll get it all sorted tomorrow.' Polly attempted to put Sarah's mind at rest, although deep down she did have niggling concern.

All the team were on the showground bright and early, including Fiona, and they were all desperately keen to get going on finishing their masterpiece.

'The Ferris wheel still isn't working correctly.'

'Let's just get on with the flower arrangements and then see if we can get it working,' ordered Elizabeth. 'I'm sure it's something and nothing.'

'I hope she knows what she's doing,' whispered Amy, who hated leaving anything until the last minute. Like Sarah, she was a meticulous planner.

'Me too, or we could all end up with egg on our faces.'

'Not me. As far as I'm concerned if it goes wrong, it's Elizabeth who has to take the blame.'

'Too true.' Sarah was amazed that she and Amy were on the same wavelength.

'I know this might shock you, Polly, but I really like Amy.' Sarah hadn't been sure whether or not to say it.

Polly smiled. 'I do too. Just goes to show that for all those years I viewed her as a rival, she's actually a pretty nice person.'

'Sorry, what was that?'

'You heard me. I like her too.'

They viewed all the buckets of flowers, agreeing that they were simply stunning. Polly felt she was in heaven. 'Aren't these all fabulous.' She took in a deep breath of the scented air.

Sarah laughed. 'OK, OK. When you've finished gushing shall we get on?'

'Let's make a start on the horses.'

The wire frame had been covered in moss, but they wanted to cover the horse's saddle with flowers, plus the mane and tail had been painstakingly fitted with hundreds of glass test tubes ready to insert the flowers into.

Sarah went round filling the tubes with water, using a bottle she'd managed to buy from a local tattoo parlour.

'Why were you there?' Polly had been surprised when

Sarah had told her where she'd bought the bottle from. 'Did you have a tattoo done?'

Sarah laughed. 'No, of course I didn't. I just know they use these special bottles with plastic straws. I saw them on a television programme.' Sarah was right. They were perfect for the job.

'I'm wondering about having a tattoo done,' Polly confessed as she stuffed moss into the small gaps.

Sarah stopped what she was doing. 'You?'

'Yes, why not?'

'What would you have?'

'I don't know. Maybe a flower or butterfly.'

'How about a slice of chocolate cake?'

'What, to eat or to have tattooed on me?' Polly laughed. 'Not sure Mark would approve of me having a piece of cake tattooed.'

'But you can't stand pain, Polly. Your pain threshold is nil.'

'That's true. Perhaps I'll just get a stick-on one. I'd love a piece of chocolate cake right now. The mention of it has sent my taste buds into overdrive.'

'Just as well you haven't got it tattooed on you, otherwise you'd be craving it all the time.'

'Ladies how are you getting on?' Elizabeth interrupted.

'Fine. We're just filling the bottles ready to put the flowers in.'

'Well, you have another four horses to do after that one,' she reminded them sharply.

'Get her. Might have known she'd start bossing us around. I don't think she's done any actual work yet other than sticking her nose into everyone's business.'

'We'd better crack on, otherwise she'll be over here again.'

It was an extremely long day, but eventually they reached the time when they could address the Ferris wheel. Amy and Chelsie had spent the day making the designs to be placed on each 'seat' of the wheel and they were looking stunning. Fiona had spent the day running around after everyone and making tea. Elizabeth, as expected, had done very little.

Everyone waited with bated breath, as Elizabeth turned on the power supply. The motor groaned and juddered. It slowly turned the turntable and the Ferris wheel began to rotate.

'It's a bit shaky,' Polly stated the obvious.

'And slow,' chipped in Fiona. 'It's like watching paint dry.'

Elizabeth glared at her, aware that this was turning into yet another disaster.

'Isn't there a switch on it for us to adjust the speed,' suggested Sarah, helpfully.

Elizabeth turned the control on the panel which was attached to the plug.

Without warning the motor fired up. The plinth rotated at such an alarming rate that Polly and Fiona had to duck so as not to be hit by the flying objects that were being propelled from the arrangement.

'Quick, quick, turn it off,' shouted Polly.

Sarah leapt into action, pushing past a rather stunned Elizabeth, and shut the machine down.

Polly burst into relieved laughter. 'Oh my God.'

'Yeah great,' said Fiona sarcastically, picking up the debris from the floor.

'There must be a way to slow it down a bit,' reasoned Sarah. She looked at the control panel. There was a centre point on it but every time she tried to get the button to stay in that position it moved. 'Quick, hand me some tape,' she ordered.

Polly pulled a small piece of sticky tape off and handed it to her. Sarah stuck the button down so it couldn't move. 'Stand back, ladies,' she said as she switched the machine on again.

Much to the relief of the group the turntable rotated at the perfect speed.

'That looks great.' Polly was thrilled.

'Yes, providing the tape doesn't come off otherwise our flower arrangement could become a lethal weapon,' laughed Fiona.

The group stood back and admired their work. It had been a long slog to get to this stage with a lot of anxieties along the way, but it was absolutely worth it to see the finished result.

All they had to do now was put the flowers in, which would take them the next two days before the exhibit was complete. Then there was the anxious overnight wait to see what award the judges decided it was worthy of.

# TWENTY-SIX

Polly and Sarah stopped in their tracks.

'What the heck is she wearing?' Polly pointed to Elizabeth.

Sarah shrugged her shoulders. Considering all the trouble they'd been through to find suitable outfits after being dictated to by Elizabeth about what they had to wear (and that's without the trauma that Polly had experienced just trying to get the jacket to fit), they couldn't believe their eyes. Elizabeth was wearing a flowery summer dress with a matching jacket. 'She looks like she's wearing her bedroom wallpaper,' Polly sneered. 'How dare she tell us what to wear when she had no intention of wearing the same thing. What a sneaky cow!'

Elizabeth was positioned in front of a television camera crew and the reporter who was keen to interview her about the design.

'Elizabeth, you and your team must be extremely thrilled with the award your design has won. It's spectacular.'

'Yes, I am very pleased.'

'How did you come up with the design?'

'Well, I always loved going to the funfair and thought it would make a fabulous subject for a floral exhibit on this scale,' she lied. 'It was a lot of hard work bringing my idea to fruition, but I think I did a very good job.'

Polly had overheard the comments and was furious. 'You designed it, Sarah – it was your idea with our input. How dare she take all the credit and not even give us a mention.'

'She wanted all the glory but didn't want to get her hands dirty.' Sarah was seething.

There was an increased amount of noise from behind Elizabeth. The TV crew, distracted by a strange groaning sound, tilted their camera towards the direction of the voice shouting, 'Stand clear!' Elizabeth was oblivious to everything except blowing her own trumpet.

The cameraman was more interested in what was unfolding behind her. The Ferris wheel had suddenly roared into life and was turning at an alarming speed. As it turned, the floral arrangements on the 'seats' started to shift. Sarah had already voiced her concerns about them not being tied down but Elizabeth had insisted that the weight of the designs would prevent them from moving. That would have been fine if the wheel had rotated at a gentle speed, but as it turned it seemed to gain momentum, with the arrangements starting to shift towards the edge of the ledges they had been placed on.

Plant material began to work its way out of the arrangements and one design that had now reached the top of the towering wheel shifted so much that it toppled over. 'Watch out,' warned an onlooker as the dish containing very wet floral foam and flowers fell off and hit a bystander right on his head.

The cameraman was laughing so much the camera wobbled. He zoomed in to get a close-up of the poor, bemused bystander, who, by now, was picking flowers out of his hair. Then he focussed the camera onto Elizabeth whose face was scarlet with embarrassment.

'Turn that thing off,' she ordered Polly. Polly was in no state to help; she was laughing so hard. A voice in the crowd had called out, 'Timberrr,' and it had proved too much for her.

Elizabeth tutted and climbed unceremoniously onto the stand. She carefully worked her way past all the other floral arrangements to reach the power point so that she could unplug the out-of-control Ferris wheel. The floral arrangements had been tightly packed onto the stand in order to disguise the cabling for the Ferris wheel, so it was quite difficult to get her tottery-heeled shoes safely between them. One of the urns was leaking. Sarah had pointed that out earlier too, but Elizabeth wasn't concerned. Now she wished she had listened to her. A pool of water had accumulated on the floor, added to which some of the foliage had shed its leaves. It left the area incredibly slippery. Elizabeth placed her foot down, painfully aware that she was now the centre of attention, but as it touched the puddle of water she slipped. There wasn't much to hold onto other than one of the pedestal arrangements. She grabbed it. Her feet slipped from underneath her and she ended up on her knees in a puddle of water with the pedestal now leaning precariously against her.

There was a gasp from the crowd, which by now had increased ten-fold to watch the ongoing palaver and record it all on their phones. Elizabeth stretched as far as she could, her dress now riding up around her bottom. She pulled out the plug to the sound of cheers and wolf whistles. The Ferris wheel finally came to a standstill. Flowers were hanging from the top of it and water was dripping all over the base. Elizabeth emerged from the stand, her knees and dress sodden. The film crew closed in on her and the reporter rushed in to help her climb off the stand. Elizabeth was in no mood to chat. Feeling totally humiliated and rather flustered, she made a hasty retreat from the marquee and fled to the nearest ladies' toilet in order to tidy herself up.

Polly and Sarah were laughing so much it hurt. They approached the reporter. 'Did you want to know any more about our design?' The reporter nodded. 'This is Sarah,' introduced Polly. 'She is the person who came up with the original idea for the funfair and got the Ferris wheel and other stands made.'

'Oh, I'm sorry, I understood Elizabeth did all that?' replied the reporter, now feeling somewhat confused.

'No, we worked as a team. Elizabeth is our team leader,' informed Sarah, not wanting to take full credit for something she hadn't done by herself.

'It was great fun,' continued Polly. 'It's lovely working as part of a team. The design starts off as an idea and with the team input, it evolves. It's just a shame that when we designed it, we hadn't taken into account that it would be standing on grass which is very uneven. It worked perfectly well when we tried it on solid ground.'

'I was going to ask you about that. I suppose the moral of the story is to try things out in situ to make sure they work well.'

'Exactly.' Sarah laughed. 'Or you could end up with it malfunctioning the way it did today.'

'Thank you, ladies, we've got enough now for our feature. It'll be on the television later today.'

Amy and Chelsie arrived, just in time to catch the end of the calamity and Elizabeth storming off.

'With all the excitement I hadn't even looked to see what we've been awarded,' laughed Polly.

'Gold medal,' squealed Chelsie.

'Well, that's made my day.'

Polly filled them in on what had happened as they were puzzled by the dishevelled state of the exhibit.

'Never a dull moment. Did they interview you?' asked Amy.

'Yes. It'll be on the TV later.'

'Do you think we'll see Elizabeth again today?'

'If I was her, I'd head for home and lock myself away until the show ends.'

'I don't believe it. Look, Elizabeth's coming back.'

Elizabeth had composed herself, or at least as much as she could considering her dress was wet right through and her knees stained from the wet foliage that she had slipped on.

'Why are you all standing around? Get this unholy mess cleared up,' she barked at them.

They all looked at her with surprise.

'I told you to tie these arrangements tightly to the Ferris wheel,' she directed at Sarah.

'No, you didn't. When I suggested that you insisted they would be fine. It's not my fault they fell off.'

'Whatever, Sarah. I'm going for a coffee.'

With that, she flounced out of the marquee leaving the team aghast.

'What a bloody nerve that woman has.'

'Let's get this mess cleared up as best we can,' suggested Amy, not wanting to get into Elizabeth's bad books any more than she already had.

Sarah picked up all the flowers that had strewn themselves across the stand whilst Polly and Chelsie started tidying up the arrangements. By the time Elizabeth had returned after her skinny latte and cinnamon bun, it was impossible to see that there had ever been an incident, apart from the odd puddle of water and the fact that the Ferris wheel was no longer turning.

Elizabeth looked furious as she stormed towards them.

'Uh oh. What's up now?' Chelsie and Amy had been enjoying manning the stand and chatting to members of the public who'd stopped by to talk and ask questions about the design. Polly and Sarah had gone to lunch so they wouldn't be back for a while.

'How dare Polly and Sarah take the credit for my design,' she spat the words out. Amy knew that Polly and Sarah had been interviewed. They had no idea what had been said, but doubted they took full credit for the design.

'They've been on the television talking about the design.'

'Oh, did they? It's great we've been given some publicity. Hopefully more people will come and have a look at it.' Amy and Chelsie suspected that their interview was probably more accurate than the one Elizabeth had given.

A few members of the public walked by, laughing and pointing at Elizabeth.

'What's their problem?'

More people started laughing and looking at the exhibit. Chelsie got her phone out and noticed that the performance of the Ferris wheel and Elizabeth scrambling around, her knickers on show, trying to switch it off was on social media and was currently the number one thing trending. More than three thousand people had viewed the video. The comments under it were hilarious.

'What is it?' Elizabeth asked, wondering what Chelsie was finding amusing.

'You're all over social media with your interview, Elizabeth.'

'Well, that's good. What's so funny?'

'It's showing the incident with the Ferris wheel and you switching it off.' She showed Elizabeth the footage. Her face turned red and without saying a word she hurried off to the security of the café, although she was sure she was the butt of everyone's jokes there too. Deciding that she couldn't put up with any more humiliation she decided to head for home.

'You two are naughty,' Amy said, as Polly and Sarah returned from lunch.

'Why, what have we done?'

'You were on the television talking about our exhibit.'

'Oh, fabulous. I hope Mark recorded it for me.'

'Elizabeth is furious with you both!'

'That doesn't surprise me at all. Where is she?'

'I think she's gone home. She was attracting an audience here. She has a lot of fans!'

'How hilarious. Dread to think what mood she'll be in tomorrow.'

Sarah felt a bit concerned as Elizabeth wasn't the easiest person to get on with anyway.

'That's if she bothers to turn up. I don't see why she can't just see the funny side of what happened. I'm sure the public would love her if she did.'

'Unfortunately, her ego has been dented.'

'I think she takes herself too seriously. If it had happened to me, I'd be laughing now,' Polly stated, although Sarah wasn't so sure. She laughed. 'I'm surprised it didn't happen to you as usually you're in the thick of any disaster.' Amy remembered the incident at the flower show a few years earlier when Polly accused her of sabotaging her work. Neither Amy nor Polly saw the funny side of that.

'OK if we go to lunch now?' Amy thought she'd change the subject.

'No problem, we've got this.'

Elizabeth was already at the stand when Polly and Sarah arrived the next day.

'Get ready for a telling-off,' said Sarah, having watched the interview when she got home.

'Hi, Elizabeth.' She was wearing a very subdued outfit, quite a contrast from the one she wore yesterday. Also, she had done something different to her hair. At a quick glance you wouldn't recognise her from the person who made such a fool of herself on the stand.

'She's changed her appearance,' noted Sarah. 'Yes, she has. Maybe so no one recognises her, especially as the video was on television last night at the end of the programme.'

Chelsie and Amy arrived and did a double take when they saw Elizabeth. They spotted Polly and Sarah and smiled.

'Hello, ladies,' said Elizabeth. 'Today should be another busy day.' She picked up a handful of brochures about the design. 'Fiona will be coming along today to lend a hand, so

I suggest you man the stand at two-hourly intervals. Is that OK?'

'Sounds good to me.'

'Sarah and Polly, do you want to begin, and Chelsie and Amy can replace you in a couple of hours? By then Fiona will be here and I'll take a break.'

Polly felt slightly uneasy working alongside Elizabeth and as soon as a member of the public showed any interest in their exhibit, she pounced on them. She didn't want to have to speak to Elizabeth. Sarah followed Polly's lead and managed to avoid Elizabeth too.

When they had their break, they decided to look around the whole show. They had been so busy focussing on their exhibit, they hadn't had a proper look around. Polly headed straight for a stall that was selling garden ornaments.

'Have you still got the dung beetle you bought for Mark?'

'Yes, but I think it's buried somewhere in the garden. It was on the lawn for ages, but I'm not sure Mark was ever impressed with it. I think he tried to lose it somewhere.' Polly had treated him to the gift when she visited a garden centre on a flower club visit to Winchester a few years earlier. 'Perhaps I should try and find something better for him this time. There were acorn bird feeders, sparkly mobiles to catch the light and unusual wire structures to enhance the garden. 'Too much choice,' said Polly. 'I just don't know what to buy for him.' This could be a lengthy process.

Dismantling the design was considerably faster than assembling it and in an extremely short time all the team's hard work was over. Most of the horses were sold to members of the public but there was one left and Polly decided to keep it for her garden. She wasn't sure what Mark's reaction would be when she arrived home, nor how she was going to get it home on the train. By the time the exhibit was cleared, and everything packed up, it was getting close to rush hour.

Polly and Sarah said their farewells to the rest of the group, and let out an audible sigh of relief that they wouldn't be working with Elizabeth again. They flagged down a taxi to take them to the station. When they arrived it was already crowded, a number of trains having been cancelled due to an earlier signalling problem.

'Bloody hell, how are we going to do this?' said Polly, who was starting to doubt her decision to rescue one of the horses.

'Our train is from platform ten.' They headed over to the platform with great difficulty as both were heavily laden with bags, shopping trolleys and a horse. A number of commuters gave her dirty looks and grumbled as she tried to fit the horse onto the train. The train was extremely crowded, with little room to stand, never mind adding several carrier bags of plant material and a metal horse to the mix.

By the time Polly and Sarah reached their station the bags of plants were decimated and Polly had imprints of the metal horse along her arms. They almost fell out of the train when the doors opened.

Mark was at the station ready to meet them. The sight of Polly struggling with the horse made him laugh out loud. 'What the hell are you doing with that?'

'I thought it would look good in our garden.' Polly's garden was barely larger than a postage stamp and was overcrowded with plants and shrubs that she used for flower arranging. Mark knew that this wasn't the time to challenge

Polly. He loaded the horse into the car and they set off. As soon as they arrived home Mark unloaded it and placed it in the middle of the back garden. It took up a considerable amount of space.

'I don't think there's going to be enough room for you to put up the washing line. I think you'll have to use this as a clothes horse now.'

'Oh, very funny.'

'It's a bit spooky, don't you think?'

'I think it looks fabulous,' Polly enthused.

# TWENTY-SEVEN

'How do you feel now that your show is over? You must be pleased with the result.'

'Relieved it's over, but it was good fun. Just don't think I could have tolerated Elizabeth for much longer.'

'It was exhausting. All those months of preparation, but the finished exhibit was wonderful.'

'Yes, apart from the Ferris wheel incident,' laughed Rose, mischievously.

'Well, it gave a lot of people a laugh. It was the number one thing trending at one time. Not sure how many people watched it but it ran into thousands.'

'How did Elizabeth feel about it?'

'Mortally embarrassed. She actually changed her appearance for the following day in the hope that no one recognised her. I think they did though. People were still laughing and pointing as they looked at the exhibit. The number one question I was asked was about the Ferris wheel malfunction,' laughed Polly.

'Now we can move onto something else and get back on track with the club.'

'I, for one, could use a holiday right now. What with work and everything else, I'm completely knackered. I've been summoned for a meeting tomorrow at work. No idea what that's all about.'

'Great news. I've lost my job.'

'Is that good?' Mark knew Polly had been unhappy for a long time but the thought of one less salary concerned him. Money was tight enough right now.

'It is. I'm getting a decent payout, so I won't have to worry about finding work for ages.'

'When you say ages, what's that mean?'

'Six months or more.'

'Don't you think it would be a good idea to look out for something now? That way you could save your redundancy payment. We could use it to pay a few bills and have a holiday.'

Polly screwed up her face and frowned. 'Suppose so, I hadn't thought about that. I was just so thrilled I don't have to work there anymore.'

'It wasn't that bad, was it?'

'Some days were OK. The main problem was that everyone was on a different wavelength to me.'

That was easy to believe. Not many people were on the same wavelength as Polly.

'Well, how about you take a month or two off, then reassess the situation.'

Polly could live with that suggestion. Mark didn't want to press Polly on it, especially as she sort of agreed to just take a couple of months off before looking for work.

This time off soon extended to three, then four months and still there was no sign that Polly had any intention of finding work. She relished being in control of her days and he could see she thrived on it. Her whole demeanour had changed, although she had replaced one stress with another, but after all, that was Polly for you. Most days now were spent baking different cakes and experimenting with recipes. Mark didn't complain initially at being Polly's Guinea pig but after discovering he couldn't do the button up on his trousers, he decided that perhaps he shouldn't be so keen to try everything she baked.

'How do I go about setting up a business?' she asked one day out of the blue.

'Are we talking about cakes? No idea. I suppose you just start selling cakes to shops. Have a look online to see if there are hints on how to do it.'

Polly quickly tapped the keys on her laptop and in a matter of seconds she had found the relevant information.

'According to this, I have to take a number of courses and maintain records. Plus, the council has to come and inspect our kitchen.'

'Sounds complicated to me.'

'Perhaps it's not such a great idea after all,' she mused.

Mark felt a little relieved that this idea was on hold. Polly battled so much with her weight and if she was baking cakes on a daily basis there would be the temptation to try everything, then get upset if she gained weight.

'How about finding some evening work in a supermarket?'

'What? Me stacking shelves?'

'Yes. Someone has to do it and I've heard that it's quite well paid.'

Polly looked at Mark. He had been a great support since she'd lost her job and she knew that money was starting to be depleted.

'Or how about getting a part-time office job. Maybe three days a week.'

'That sounds like it might work.'

'You don't sound too enthusiastic.'

'No, I'm not. Not really. I'll see what I can do.'

It made sense. Most of Polly's friends went to work so she wasn't doing a great deal during the daytime, other than watching television.

'How about seeing if you can get a job in a bakery or a florist.'

'Now that's an idea. I think the florist in the high street is offering part-time work. I might pop in and ask.'

Polly felt upbeat at the prospect of doing something she loved to earn money. Anything was better than working in an office as far as she was concerned.

Polly hadn't been for an interview in years and certainly wasn't expecting the formal way Hannah conducted it. She felt a mixture of nervousness and excitement.

'Have you worked in floristry before?'

'No, but I love flowers and run a flower club.'

Hannah seemed quite impressed. As she was considering Polly, she gathered up a selection of flowers from the many buckets she had in the shop.

She handed them to Polly. 'I'd like you to make a hand-tied bouquet.'

The colour drained from Polly's face. 'What? Now?'

'Yes. If you're going to work here, I need to know you can make these quickly as we sell a huge number of orders on a daily basis.'

Polly stripped away the surplus leaves and attempted to

spiral the flowers. It was extremely slow going especially as Hannah was watching every move and talking to her.

'Sorry,' stuttered Polly. 'I just feel nervous with you watching me.'

'I don't mean to,' replied Hannah. 'Try to forget I'm here.'

She took a few paces back, so she was no longer breathing down Polly's neck. After what seemed like forever, Polly was holding something that, at a stretch, could be considered to be a hand-tied bouquet.

Polly did her best. Hannah inspected her work, then slammed the stems on the table and let go, in order to see if it would stand up by itself. It just about managed to do so providing no one knocked the table. She trimmed the stems slightly until it stood up perfectly, then let out a sigh of relief.

Hannah passed her a sheet of tissue paper and cellophane. 'If you could wrap it now please.'

She was all fingers and thumbs as she attempted to tie the cellophane in place. Hannah could see her struggling and offered a hand to help.

'Can I have some sticky tape, please?'

'We always use string for this.' She handed her a length of string to tie the cellophane around the bouquet. After a bit of a battle the bouquet was sitting on the table, complete.

'Not bad. You just need to speed up a bit and relax. It's not that difficult really.'

'If you say so,' laughed Polly. 'I'm more used to doing arrangements.'

'Well, we might need you to do those as well.'

'Does this mean that I've got the job?'

'Yes. You can start next Monday. Be here at eight.'

Polly tried not to show her shock at needing to be at work so early. She'd got into a lazy habit of getting up around nine every day now.

'OK.'

'Can you do Monday and Wednesday?' asked Hannah.

'That's great, thanks.' She couldn't wait to get home to tell Mark.

'Eight o'clock?' shrieked Mark. 'Well, this should certainly be interesting.' He grinned.

'Alright, alright. I know I enjoy my lie-in every day.'

'Still, it's great you're going to be earning some money and doing something you love.'

'True. Just hope not many people want bouquets in a hurry.'

Mark was always up by seven. Polly would normally turn over and go back to sleep for an hour or two. But she was determined to prove Mark wrong and set two alarms in case she didn't hear the first one. She needn't have bothered. Mark made a point of waking her when he got out of bed.

'Rise and shine, sleepy head.'

The night had gone by quickly and Polly awoke feeling that she'd only just fallen asleep. Dreams about flowers had kept her from relaxing properly. She reluctantly got up, wishing she could catch just a few more minutes in bed. In no time she was washed and dressed and heading to her car.

'Have a good day,' Mark called out. She smiled nervously. Despite Polly's experience in flower arranging, she wasn't too sure about working as a florist.

A vast array of flowers and foliage greeted Polly, which had just been delivered by the "Dutch Man".

'Morning, Polly. If you could start by getting all this conditioned, that would be good.' She pointed to the shed at the back of the shop. 'There are buckets there and a water tap. Leave everything in there when you've finished.'

Polly followed her instructions. She set about cutting the stems from all the flowers and removing the unwanted leaves before placing them in buckets of water.

She was gasping for a drink but didn't dare ask for one as everyone seemed far too busy.

'I've done that. What would you like me to do now?' she asked, as she stepped back into the shop.

'Great.' Hannah handed her a stack of written orders. 'Can you deal with these? They're all bouquets.' Polly could feel her stomach churning but tried to appear calm.

Hannah handed her a colour brochure. 'The bouquets are in this brochure. All you have to do is follow the instructions. Your bouquets should look like these photos when they're finished.'

That sounded easy to Polly. At least she had something to copy.

The first order was for a regular-sized bouquet of pink and purple flowers. She gathered up the flowers as per the list, a bit like pulling together all the ingredients for a cake.

Two pink roses, one pink gerbera, two stems of purple lisianthus, two sprays of pink chrysanthemum and three carnations, plus two pieces of eucalyptus.

No matter how hard Polly tried she couldn't make it look like the one in the picture. 'It needs more flowers,' she insisted.

'Yes, it does,' agreed Hannah, 'but if you add anything more that's my profit disappearing. Just try to shoosh out the flowers to make the bouquet look bigger.' Polly did her best, and Hannah reluctantly accepted it, even though it wasn't up to the usual standard, but Polly had taken so long, at this rate she'd never get finished.

'Try to speed up a bit, Polly. The more you do the easier it will get.'

'OK. Sorry.' Polly wasn't convinced. She could feel herself panicking. Aware that Hannah was watching her, she fumbled with the flowers in her hand, dropping one or two.

'Be careful,' called Hannah from across the shop. This only made Polly feel worse. Tears were starting to well up in her eyes and she realised she wasn't cut out to be a florist. She scrutinised the flowers in front of her and admitted defeat.

'I'm sorry, Hannah. I just can't do this when I'm under pressure.'

Hannah tried to appear sympathetic but, deep down, she was trying to hide her annoyance.

'Perhaps floristry isn't for you,' she said, trying to be as tactful as possible.

'Are you firing me?' Polly seemed shocked.

'Well, we need help making bouquets, and if you can't make them, then I'm afraid,' she paused before continuing, 'there's no easy way to say this, Polly, but I'll have to let you go.'

Hannah opened the till and handed Polly a crisp twenty-pound note.

'I'd better get my coat then.' She took the money, grabbed her coat and fled. Just as she was getting into her car her phone rang.

'Hiya,' came Mark's cheerful voice. 'How's it going?'

'I've been fired.'

There was a pause.

'You what?'

'They fired me because I couldn't make the hand-tied bouquets fast enough.'

Mark laughed. 'Now I've heard everything.'

'To think I got up at the crack of dawn to get here. I'm cold, tired and unemployed.'

'Look at the positive side. You don't have to get up early tomorrow.'

'Suppose so.' Polly felt embarrassed. 'What will I tell everyone?'

'Who did you tell that you were working there?'

'Sarah, Maggie, the usual suspects.'

'Tell them you had a difference of opinion, and you didn't want to compromise.'

'Sounds good. I'll tell them that we parted because of creative differences. I'm going home to bed.'


'Did you get fired?' asked Lizzy.

'No,' lied Polly. 'I realised I couldn't work somewhere like that.'

'Like what? It was only a florist's, not an abattoir or animal testing centre.'

Rose laughed. She suspected the real reason was that Polly struggled to make hand-tied bouquets.

Polly blushed. 'OK, OK. I was too slow making hand-tieds. Plus, I wanted to add extra flowers to make them look nice.'

'So, basically, she fired you because she couldn't afford to keep you on?'

'Something like that.'

'I get the feeling I'm never going to find work. There's no way I'm going to go back to working in an office.'

'Something will turn up.'

'Shall we get on?' interrupted Sarah. She knew Polly only too well and had doubted she'd survive in a florist's shop anyway.

'Let's talk about our next club meeting. What are we going to do?'

'Who fancies demonstrating?' Sarah asked.

'I've been asked to do a couple of demonstrations.'

'Who? Where?' Lizzy was gobsmacked. She knew Polly was good at arranging flowers, but also knew she hated standing up in front of anyone. It had been close to impossible to persuade her to do a demonstration at her own club.

'Don't sound so surprised.'

'Where?'

'Greenwood flower club and Crossfield horticultural society. What on earth am I going to do?' Polly felt flattered to be asked, but worried at the same time.

'You'll be fine,' Rose tried to reassure her. 'Do something you're comfortable with.'

'What? Make cakes?' Lizzy asked innocently. 'But they've come to see flowers.'

'Yes, but you could make a cake which they can enjoy whilst you're arranging the flowers.'

'Yes. Distract them from the flower arrangements.' Lizzy blurted out.

Polly glared at her, feeling hurt. 'Sorry, I didn't mean it like that.' Lizzy tried to scramble out of the hole she was digging, but it seemed to be getting deeper.

'It'll be fun. An evening of cake and flowers.' Rose attempted to calm the situation. She could tell that Polly was upset and even more worried now after Lizzy's comment.

'Any chance we can get back to what we're doing?' asked Sarah who was keen to keep everyone on track.

'I'm happy to do something,' Rose volunteered. 'How about a parallel design?'

'I think that's my favourite design and relatively straightforward for our members to attempt,' said Polly, pleased that she didn't have to do the demonstration. She knew she was going to be far too stressed planning her own demonstrations. 'Are you OK to sort that, Rose?'

'No problem, leave it with me,' reassuring Polly that she had the situation under control.

# TWENTY-EIGHT

'What are you up to?' Mark was surprised to see the kitchen in total chaos when he'd arrived home from work.

'I'm baking cakes for my flower dem tomorrow.'

'I thought they booked you to do flower arrangements.'

'Not you as well. Lizzy said that. She thought it would distract them from my flower arranging.'

'That doesn't sound like a compliment.'

'I'm not sure it was meant to be. Who knows with Lizzy. She has a habit of speaking before engaging her brain. But I think it'll be fun.'

'Oh, OK.' Mark wasn't too sure he understood but decided to leave Polly to it. There were some things he'd never understand.

Once Polly had the cakes all sliced up and carefully packed into tins and boxes, she set about loading them into the car. Followed by various buckets and containers filled with flowers. It was a tight squeeze, but she was happy everything was secure and off she went. Mark was left to clear up the disaster in the kitchen. Not that he complained.

Polly had left him a couple of slices of lemon drizzle cake as a reward.

Polly carried the boxes through into the church hall. The ladies in the hall seemed surprised to see her.

'Hello, Polly.' It was Anna, the club secretary.

'Hi. Where shall I put all my stuff? I'm parked on double yellows, so if someone can help me unload that would be good.'

She looked bemused. 'Oh, Polly, it's not tonight.'

'What do you mean? I've got it in my diary.'

'It's next year.'

Polly was stunned for a second. 'What? No, we discussed it and agreed it was tonight.'

'I'm so sorry. I don't know what to say. I feel terrible about it.'

Not as awful as Polly felt. She'd stressed all day getting everything ready.

'But I've bought all these flowers and baked a load of cakes.'

Some of the ladies' eyes lit up at the mention of cakes.

'We'll happily help eat those.'

Polly thought for a second and caught a glimpse of the traffic warden out of the corner of her eye.

'Got to go.' She rushed outside.

'Please don't,' she shouted to the traffic warden.

'Is this your car?'

'Yes.'

'You can't park here.'

'I was only unloading.'

The warden handed her a parking fine.

'Please, I'm having a terrible evening.' Polly started to relay the events of the evening to him.

'I'm sorry, love. I can't cancel the ticket. You'll have to appeal, although I'm not sure they'll accept your explanation.'

Polly started to get emotional. The tiredness and stress from the day was catching up with her, and she started to cry.

A policeman was passing and stopped to check what the problem was. Polly recognised him. He was the policeman who'd caught her doing a little "community pruning" a couple of years earlier.

'Is there a problem?'

The warden explained the situation and walked off in search of another illegally parked car.

'I was sure I knew you from somewhere. Now I remember, you're the lady who pinches foliage.'

Polly tried to stop the tears but by now they were rolling uncontrollably down her cheeks.

'Community pruning, to be precise.'

The policeman smiled. 'Oh yes. Community pruning.'

'Tonight's cost me over a hundred pounds. I've got a car full of flowers, a hundred cakes and now a parking fine.'

The policeman looked into the car. 'Those cakes look delicious.' He could almost hear them calling to him as he peered into the plastic containers.

'I have an idea. Will the cakes keep fresh until tomorrow?'

'Absolutely.'

'Great. Move your car over there so you won't have it towed away and follow me.'

Polly followed the policeman into the police station around the corner, both of them laden with stacks of cake boxes.

He set a tray of cakes on the counter. 'I think I may have solved our problem.' He beamed at his colleagues. 'This lady has a car full of surplus cakes and flowers for sale.'

'Great,' said the sergeant. 'We've a bit of a *do* tomorrow for some VIPs and our caterer has let us down. They look amazing.'

'She has a hundred of these plus loads of flowers.'

'Even better. That means we can all have a cake too. Can we buy them from you? Would you be able to do a few bouquets for us to give out?'

'Sure can. Could I drop them off in the morning? I'd like to wrap them and all my stuff is at home.'

After some discussion the flowers for the bouquets were chosen.

'I'll buy some of these for the missus.'

'Me too, though she'll wonder why.'


Polly left the station feeling very pleased with herself. What had started out as a disaster had become a success and she'd got a pocketful of money into the bargain. Then she remembered her parking fine, which brought her rapidly back down to earth.

# TWENTY-NINE

The day had arrived for Polly's next flower demonstration. She had checked and double-checked that she had the correct day, and the correct year after the last fiasco.

Polly placed the dish on top of the container. She looked nervously at the audience. There was momentary silence; that awkward silence which was hard to break. All eyes were on her. She took a deep breath.

'Ladies, let's begin. I'm placing some garden foliage first.' She picked up her brand-new pair of florist scissors and nipped the end of one of her fingers. She tried not to react, despite it hurting. She continued, trying to hide the fact that blood was dripping onto the foliage and container.

'Excuse me. Your finger's bleeding,' shouted someone in the audience.

'Oh yes.' Polly tried to make out she hadn't noticed. She wrapped a tissue around her finger. 'I've got a plaster,' came a voice from the back of the room. Polly looked where the voice had come from. 'Thank you.' The plaster was passed down the hall until a member of the audience handed it to

Polly. It had clearly seen better days, but at least it would do the trick for now. She stuck it to her finger and continued.

'What's that foliage you're using?' asked a member of the audience. Polly didn't really know, after all, she had pinched it from her neighbour's garden. She would often prune some of the foliage that hung over the fence as her neighbour seemed to grow some interesting plants.

Mark had stood guard whilst Polly tried to cut some of the pieces of a particularly interesting shrub which was just out of her reach. On tiptoe, Polly stretched as far as she could to reach it, but no matter how hard she tried she couldn't quite get hold of it. Spotting one of her flower pots, she moved it close to the fence so she could stand on it.

'Careful,' shouted Mark.

'I'm almost there.'

No sooner had the words left her mouth than she lost her balance and, where the ivy that covered the fence had weakened it, the fence gave way and Polly ended up sprawled on top of it. 'Help,' she called.

Mark fell about with laughter. 'You do look a sight, Polly.' He took his phone out of his pocket and snapped a photo.

'Well, don't just stand there. Help me up,' she cried.

Mark took her hand and tried to get her onto her feet. Polly's jeans snagged on an old rusty nail on the fence panel. The more Mark tried to get Polly to her feet, the more the nail tore her jeans. 'Bloody hell,' remarked Mark.

'What?' Polly was still face down on top of the fence panel.

'Helen and Andrew are back.'

'Oh my God, what's happened here?' shrieked Helen, wondering why Polly was spreadeagled in her garden.

'I was trying to clear some of the ivy on the fence and it collapsed,' Polly lied.

'Andrew, help Mark get Polly off my garden.' Between them they managed to get Polly to her feet. They lifted the fence panel to reveal some very squashed geranium which Helen had planted only the day before.

'Look at my geraniums. They're ruined,' cried Helen.

'I'm so sorry,' sobbed Polly. 'It was an accident.'

'We'll replace them, of course.' insisted Mark. 'You will. And the fence,' shouted Helen as she headed indoors, looking very distressed.

Mark, his mouth set in a hard line, raised his eyebrows. 'That's an expensive lesson. Not only have we to replace the fence panel and Helen's precious geraniums, but you didn't even get the foliage you wanted. And your new jeans are ruined.' Polly really tried Mark's patience at times.

Nowadays Polly was a bit more careful. She only cut foliage that was hanging in her own garden, but she still couldn't identify half of it. 'It's just various garden foliage, sorry I don't know the name,' she continued.

By the time she had placed some carnations and roses in the design it looked quite pretty and she got a round of applause from the audience.

On to the next design. Polly placed a dish in the top of her container and began. It was only after she had started placing foliage and flowers into the design that she realised she was using the wrong dish. The one she meant to use was slightly larger. After the disaster with the cut finger, she decided to say nothing and continue. Everything was going well and the design was coming along a treat until the dish slipped and the design started to list. Polly tried to correct it, but as she did it slipped further down into the container. There was a gasp from the audience. Polly lifted the container and tilted it in the hope of retrieving her arrangement. It didn't work. She tipped the container upside down and the whole arrangement fell out onto the table. Luckily most of the plant material was still in place and having righted it she tidied it up and placed the dish on the bottom of the upturned container. There was a cheer and round of applause for her saving it.

Surely nothing else could go wrong this evening. She began to think that she wasn't really cut out to do flower demonstrations. She had no idea they would be this stressful.

At least the evening couldn't get any worse, or so she thought. She'd fished out a fairly old pair of tights to wear that evening along with a new dress she'd been itching to wear but had never seemed to have an opportunity.

'Looking good Mrs,' Mark had commented as she descended the stairs.

'I'm really pleased with it.' She smiled, slipping on her ankle boots. She stretched out her legs in a strange unfeminine way.

Mark laughed. 'What the—?'

'These bloody tights! They keep slipping down.' Polly raised her dress and hitched them up.

She'd forgotten about this, what with the near disaster that evening, but she was suddenly aware, very aware, that her tights were sliding down and, more worryingly, they were taking her knickers with them.

She froze on the spot. Trying to carry on with her design as though nothing untoward was happening, she couldn't help thinking that any sudden movement could cause her underwear to end up round her ankles.

She paused for a second and placed her hands in her dress pockets in the hope of being able to hoist up the tights again. It worked, temporarily, but definitely wasn't going to resolve the situation. She knew that somehow she had to continue and finish the design. She rushed through the final part of the arrangement and carefully carried it across the room to display it on the table.

She wasn't sure if the audience wondered why she was shuffling along the floor, but that was the only way she dared to walk. It was such a relief when everyone headed for the refreshment table and she could head into the ladies' toilets to adjust her underwear.

The second half of the evening passed with no drama whatsoever. Polly found it hard to believe it could be so easy, but in many ways, she was relieved when it was all over. She didn't think her nerves could take much more.

'How'd it go?' called out Mark. 'Were they expecting you this evening?'

'Yes, fine.' Polly knew he was having a playful dig at her after the last time.

'Did it go OK?'

'Well, apart from the fact that I cut my finger, one of my designs slipped to the bottom of the container and I had to tip it upside down to retrieve it, and my knickers nearly fell down, everything was fine.'

Mark was beside himself. He couldn't stop laughing. 'Not sure you're cut out for this flower demonstrating lark.'

'Me neither,' laughed Polly. Ever hopeful that next time, if there was a next time, everything would be fine.

# THIRTY

Polly was busy filling in the committee about the saga of the demonstration and everything that had gone wrong.

'At least you got the right day this time,' teased Rose.

'Yes, that was a result.' Lizzy started laughing. 'What's so funny?' asked Polly.

'Just thinking of you and your knickers falling down, it reminded me of a friend who was at the Notting Hill Carnival one year. She was dressed scantily in little more than a bra and knickers and she had a serious wardrobe malfunction.'

'Really? What happened?' Polly was curious to know.

'Her bra snapped as she was dancing in the middle of the road. Everyone got a real eyeful!'

'How dreadful,' Polly was laughing. 'What did she do?'

'She grabbed her boobs, climbed onto one of the floats and hid behind some scenery until they reached a toilet. She jumped the queue to get it sorted out. Fortunately, someone was able to come to the rescue with a number of safety pins.'

'Oh God. How embarrassing. I'd have been mortified if

that ever happened to me.' Sarah hated being the centre of attention.

'It was, but she laughs about it now. At least no one was aware of your predicament, Polly.' Maggie knew that Polly had had a lucky escape and that it could have been so much worse.

'The next time you do a dem, make sure you're wearing a pair of tights that fit and knickers that haven't lost their elasticity,' suggested Sarah, helpfully.

'I'm not sure we should ask Polly to do the dem at our club meeting on Saturday,' Maggie commented.

'Are you offering?'

'OK, I'll do it,' confirmed Maggie.

'Just make sure you wear knickers with tight elastic, we don't want any wardrobe malfunctions, do we?' laughed Sarah.

It was unlikely Polly would ever be allowed to forget her first flower demonstration.

'So, what are we going to do?'

'How about a traditional triangle this time. It's a good design to learn,' suggested Maggie.

'Yes, but they take quite a lot of flowers.' Polly was wary of overspending.

'I'm not thinking about a pedestal, just something small. We'd only need a bit of foliage, a bunch of roses, and a filler flower. That should suffice. I can probably get them all from the supermarket and save a bit of money.'

'So, we're decided then? We'll do that?' Polly noticed that Lizzy wasn't paying much attention, which was nothing new.

'What are you thinking, Lizzy?'

'I'm just wondering if there's an update on the love triangle.'

Polly didn't admit it, but she'd thought a lot about that since it all came to light.

'Well, we've only got a few days to wait, then no doubt we'll get the next instalment.'

'How are things?' Polly was relieved that she'd got to Angela and Suzy before Lizzy had.

Angela gave a sad smile. 'We're working on it.' She glanced at Suzy.

A younger woman was with them. 'This is Debbie, Derek's third wife.'

'No!' Polly's mouth dropped open.

'We thought Debbie should come to the flower club with us.'

'Yes, looks like I'm Mrs. Gullible number three. I know him as David.'

'Have you got children too?'

'No. Thank God.'

'He said he loves us all and can't choose between us.'

'What a rotter. I can't believe it.'

'No, neither could we.'

'How long have you been with him, Debbie?'

'Almost five years. Can you believe it? He told me he was working on an oil rig. That's why he disappeared a lot. I had no idea he had two other families.'

'I take it he's not living with any of you?'

'It's complicated. We're sorting out child support and visitation rights. I don't want the kids to suffer.'

'Oh, absolutely. I'm still gobsmacked.'

Lizzy was a bit miffed that Polly had got there first. She was attempting to lip-read from the other side of the hall.

This month, she was running the sales table to raise funds for the club. She was itching to find out what was happening and how much Polly knew.

Polly felt important, knowing some scandal before Lizzy. She knew she'd have to tell her in due course, but decided to savour the moment for as long as she could.

'Well?' whispered Lizzy, conspiratorially.

'You see that woman there.' Polly pointed surreptitiously towards Debbie.

'Yes.'

'She's wife number three.' Polly walked away, leaving Lizzy stunned and desperate for more information.

'Welcome, everyone. Shall we begin?' Polly called everyone to order. Lizzy would have to wait a bit longer before she got the whole story.

The committee meetings seemed to come around quickly, although it probably felt that way because Rose and Lizzy were now on two committees. Lizzy couldn't believe the amount of gossip that seemed to generate from the flower clubs. What with Angela and Suzy, and now Debbie, but she was curious about Freda's mystery man.

'How's your fella, Freda?'

'OK I think.' She hesitated. 'I expected him to come over last week but when I got to the airport to meet him he didn't appear. He'd missed the flight. Apparently, he had the wrong paperwork.'

'Don't tell me. He wants you to send more money.'

'Well, yes, he does. The visa he had was the wrong one and to get another one through quickly he needs to pay a supplement.'

'Don't send it. George and I think he's a con man.'

Freda was shocked. 'Why are you and your husband discussing my private life?'

'We don't want you to get hurt.'

Freda had felt a niggling doubt once or twice but had chosen to ignore it. She knew that some people thought she was a bit stupid.

'How much have you sent him now?' Lizzy didn't beat about the bush.

'Probably about five thousand pounds now.'

'You're mad,' shrieked Edna.

Freda looked embarrassed and close to tears.

'No, she's not.' Rose tried to calm the situation.

'What exactly do you know about him? Does he work? Where does he live?' Edna interrogated Freda.

'He lives in Morocco with his mother who he looks after,' interjected Rose.

'If that's the case, why would he want to leave her to come here?'

'Perhaps he needs to earn money to send home.'

'Yes, but he won't be allowed to work.'

'Can we get on?' Edna didn't have time for this.

'We're just trying to help Freda.'

'Well, can you do it in your own time? We've got a lot to get through this evening.'

Rose glared at her and glanced at Lizzy. 'Don't worry, Freda. Lizzy and I will help you get to the bottom of this.'

Freda looked relieved but still felt a little uncomfortable.

'Right, ladies. On to more *important* things.' Edna sounded patronising. 'Who is on the rota to make cakes this month for our members?'

Freda got home from the committee meeting feeling quite deflated. She might have guessed everyone would have an opinion. What right did they have to stick their noses into her business?

She immediately logged online and checked her messages. As hoped, there was one waiting for her from Mo. It immediately cheered her up. He was making plans to visit her and had booked his ticket. Hopefully, this time, everything would run smoothly. She couldn't wait to let Edna and the rest of the committee see her with her young man on her arm.

'I've been doing some research and I think Freda's toy boy is taking her for a ride,' Lizzy blurted down the phone to Rose.

'Right. Research, you say. What did you discover?'

'There's someone who goes by the same name and looks identical to the photo Freda showed us. In fact, this person is all over with photos of himself and his family. When I checked his profile it was legit but it bore no resemblance to the story Freda's fella had told her.'

'So, anyway, I messaged this bloke.'

'And?'

'He's never heard of Freda. He is happily married. He said his social media account was recently compromised.'

'She must go to the police with this. Maybe they can do something to get her money back.'

'I'm not so sure. Until she accepts this is a scam, I doubt anyone can help her.'

'Oh no. I had wondered. We have to tell her that she's been conned.'

'She said he's arriving next week from Morocco.'

'Well, I think we need to go along to the airport to see if he turns up.'

Lizzy was bursting with excitement, but without a car she knew she would need to involve Polly.

'Rose, how come I didn't know about Freda?' Polly felt slightly miffed that she was out of the loop.

'Has Lizzy said something?'

'She might have let slip.'

'I might have guessed she would be blabbing this everywhere. We promised Freda we wouldn't say anything to anyone. She'd be horrified.'

'I bet she would,' chipped in Sarah.

'Don't tell me you know you too?'

'Of course. Polly told me.'

Rose laughed. 'No one can keep secrets around here, can they?'

'Has she figured out who this man is?'

'No. She's still adamant that he's genuine. Lizzy thinks Freda's been catfished.'

'What on earth's that?'

'Someone has been pretending to be someone else to communicate with her.'

'How awful. I do hope for Freda's sake that if that's true then at the very least she gets her money back. I feel really sorry for her.'

'Well, don't say anything to her. I think it'll make matters worse for her. It's best we just forget about this conversation.'

'Don't worry, I won't tell anyone,' Polly fibbed. She knew perfectly well she would be filling Mark in on all the details later.

'I'm going to head to the airport when he's due to arrive.'

'Does Freda know you're going?' asked Polly.

'I'm actually taking her there.' Polly knew that Rose was probably the best person to drive Freda to the airport.

'Lizzy has asked me for a lift to the airport.' Polly felt a bit embarrassed about telling Rose this after her reaction to her knowing about the situation.

'Please tell me she's not coming.'

The doorbell rang. 'You can ask her yourself,' Polly said over her shoulder as she went to the front door to let Lizzy in.

'Are we all set for Thursday?' she asked Polly before even taking her coat off.

'Lizzy, I don't think you should go,' shouted Rose from the lounge. Lizzy pulled a face. 'Why not? You're going.'

'Yes, but I'm taking Freda. She's embarrassed enough about all this, especially if, as we suspect, he's a fraud.'

'We can go incognito,' suggested Polly. Nothing or no one was going to stop her from heading to the airport. She lived and breathed for a scandal. 'You won't even know we're there.'

'Like the time you spied on me and my blind date?' Sarah teased.

Polly had pretty much given the game away when she was hiding behind some pot plants at the garden centre where Sarah was meeting her mystery man. She stood out like a sore thumb.

'We'll just come along for support and if we're not needed then we'll quietly slip away. Freda has no need to know that we were ever there.'

Rose wasn't convinced but she knew that when Polly and Lizzy had an idea, they were unlikely to be dissuaded, especially on something as intriguing as this.

'Can we get on with the meeting now?' suggested Rose who was starting to get annoyed with the whole situation.

It was clear that no one was really concentrating on the meeting and had little to say about the next club meeting. Everyone was more interested in the Freda situation.

No sooner had everyone left than Polly headed into the spare room where Mark was working. He looked up from his computer as Polly related the whole story.

'Good grief. What is it with you lot?'

'What d'you mean?'

'Freda's involved with a potential scammer, there are three women all married to the same man. My life looks pretty tame compared to this. I think I need to join a flower club.'

'Boring, you mean?' Polly laughed.

'Yes. Boring. Give me boring any day. At least I don't have to look over my shoulder all the time.'

# THIRTY-ONE

'I wondered if you fancied going to the cinema tonight,' suggested Mark. 'There's a new film out that's supposed to be good. I've managed to get hold of a couple of promotional tickets from work.' It had been a long time since he and Polly had gone out together.

'Can't tonight, I'm afraid. I'm going to the airport to see if Freda's boyfriend turns up. He's supposed to be arriving on a flight this evening.'

'You're going to spy on her!'

'Not exactly. We're going to support her if it all goes sour.'

'Does she know you're going?'

'No.'

'So you *are* going to spy on her.'

'Well, if you put it that way, yes.'

'You're unreal. Why can't you just let her get on with her life?'

'We're worried about her.'

Mark knew that Polly was concerned about Freda, but he also knew how nosy she was and how she hated being left out of any scandal or gossip.

'Just as long as you know what you're doing.'

'We'll stay in the background and just appear if there's an issue. Don't you worry. We've got it all planned.'

'So I guess I'll be heading to the cinema on my own?'

'Sorry, it looks that way. Got to get ready or we'll miss the flight arriving.'

Mark realised there was little he could say to change Polly's mind, so he left her to it and looked forward to hearing the full story on her return.

Freda felt nervous and excited whilst getting ready. Rose had implied that she knew this man was a fraud, but something stopped Freda from believing. She couldn't admit that she'd been taken for a ride. She was hoping to prove her doubters wrong and shut them up once and for all.

Polly, Sarah and Lizzy arrived at the airport in plenty time. They wanted to get settled before Freda and Rose arrived.

Having checked the arrivals board, they decided to get coffee whilst they waited. They spotted a café that had a good view of the meeting point. Sarah went and got some drinks for them.

'Bloody hell, what a rip off,' she complained as she put the drinks on the table. 'These drinks are so expensive, especially yours, Polly.' Polly drank very weak black tea, so it was an expensive cup of hot water.

After a short while Polly spotted Freda and Rose at the meeting point. Rose looked around.

'Everything OK, Rose?' Rose appeared more nervous than Freda.

'Fine,' she lied. She didn't want to bump into Polly. She'd caught a glimpse of Polly out of the corner of her eye, or at least she assumed it was Polly. Someone was wearing an extremely colourful shirt, identical to one that Polly often wore. Polly hadn't given her wardrobe much consideration, but now she wished that she'd worn something a bit more discreet.

'Let's get a cuppa,' suggested Rose as she ushered Freda in the opposite direction from where Polly was.

'Have you thought what you're going to do if he doesn't turn up?'

'Not really.' Freda started welling up with tears. 'If I've been taken for a fool, I don't know how I can ever look anyone in the eye again. And all that money.'

'Let's not worry now. We can cross that bridge if we come to it.'

The flight number appeared on the arrivals board and passengers started to appear from the customs hall. Freda held up a sign with Mo's name on it. She scrutinised everyone who came through.

Polly, Lizzy and Sarah watched intently from the coffee shop and wondered if the mystery man would appear.

Freda was beside herself. She felt like such a fool. The realisation that Mo might not appear was starting to dawn on her, but she simply didn't want to believe it.

'There must be a mistake. I'm sure he's coming.'

'We've been waiting for more than an hour and everyone on the flight has long gone. I don't think he'll turn up now. Let's get online to see if he's sent any messages.'

Rose sat Freda down with a cup of tea, sweetened in order to deal with the shock of Mo not appearing. She powered up her tablet for Freda to use. Having logged into her account, Freda checked her messages. There was nothing as such from Mo, however there was an email from a different email address. She opened it and couldn't believe what she read.

It was from someone called Mo, who claimed that the Mo that had been communicating with her was actually someone called Al. Mo had recently discovered that his account had been hacked and someone was using his personal details. To make matters worse, it turned out to be his uncle. He left a phone number for Freda to call.

Freda felt sick. How could she have been such an idiot? The photo Mo had sent of Al showed a much older man, twice the weight and nothing at all like the person Freda had fallen for.

Rose dialled up the number given and in a second or two Mo was on a video call with them. He was a young man, the same man as on the photo that had previously been sent to Freda.

'I'm so sorry my uncle has tricked you. I'm furious with him.'

'He seemed so genuine.'

'If it's any consolation you are not the only person he has fooled.'

'That doesn't make it better,' replied Rose on Freda's behalf.

'I sent him a lot of money. I can't believe how stupid I was.'

'Is there any way we can contact him?' asked Rose, in the hope that they could get some of the money back.

'He's here now. I'll get him.'

'Well, I never. Looks like we're going to get the story straight from the horse's mouth,' said Rose. Freda was shaking nervously.

Mo disappeared from the screen and they could hear a lot of shouting in a language neither recognised. Eventually an elderly man appeared. 'Hello,' he said. 'I'm Al.'

'Is that all you have to say?' snapped Freda.

'What have you got to say for yourself?' interrupted Rose. 'At what point did you think it was OK to con Freda out of money. Worst of all you impersonated your nephew to do it.'

'I believed you. I thought I was helping a genuine person who cared about me, when all the time you're a nasty, scheming, heartless bastard,' Freda hissed, before Al could get a word in.

Rose was slightly shocked by Freda's language. She'd never heard her speak like that before, but if ever there was an occasion to use language like this, it was now.

'I am sorry.' Al tried to sound sincere.

'That's not good enough. Are you going to return the money?'

'I can't. I don't have it.'

'He will,' butted in Mo. 'I will make sure he does, but it will take time.'

'Why did you take my money and let me believe you were a decent human being? How wrong could I have been? I don't ever want to see your lying face again.'

Freda got up and walked off before Al had a chance to reply. Right now she wasn't prepared to listen to anything he had to say.

'You make sure you transfer the money over. Freda is a kind lady who doesn't deserve to be treated like this,' Rose reiterated.

'Don't worry. We will get her money back somehow.'

'As long as you aren't going to scam someone else.'

'He will not, or at least, not using my photo and details.'

The call ended.

Polly, Lizzy and Sarah had all been watching from afar and couldn't understand what was going on. Curiosity got the better of them and they made a beeline for Rose who filled them in.

'Where's Freda now?'

They looked around and could see her propping up the bar.

They headed over and joined her. 'Didn't know you drank, Freda?'

'I don't normally but I needed one. She held up her G&T. Cheers!'

'Can I join you?' asked Rose.

She looked round and saw Sarah, Polly and Lizzy standing there.

'What are you doing here? Come to gloat, have you?'

'No, we were worried about you.' Sarah gently held Freda's hand. 'Are you OK?'

'You were right. All of you. You said I was being a fool and I was.'

'No one said that. You are a lovely person, and we care about you. It's just that there are some wicked people out there.'

'Mo has promised he'll get the money back to you somehow.'

'It's not all about the money. I genuinely believed someone found me interesting and wanted to hear what I had to say.'

'*We* find you interesting. It's just that you met a scumbag. That's all.'

'This isn't about you. He is the one at fault here.' Rose tried to reassure her. 'There's not a wicked bone in your body.'

'Karma will get him. What goes around, comes around. Isn't that true?' asked Polly, who was a firm believer in this.

'Absolutely.' Whilst Lizzy loved a bit of juicy gossip, on this occasion she decided to reign herself in. She really felt bad for Freda and could guess that Edna would thrive on the outcome of this.

'I don't know about you, but I could do with a drink too. Another G&T, Freda?'

It was very late when Polly arrived home. Mark had already gone to bed. Polly was bursting to tell him what happened. She nudged him as she got into bed.

'You awake?'

'I am now, thank you.'

'You'll never guess what.'

'He didn't turn up.'

'How do you know?'

'Just a hunch.'

'When he didn't show up, Rose got onto her computer and tracked him down. Turns out Mo's uncle had hacked his account.'

'How did Freda take the news?'

'As you'd expect. She was devastated, so we stayed and had a drink or two with her in the bar.'

'Is that why you're home so late?'

'We couldn't just abandon her in her hour of need.'

'No, I suppose not. What about the money she gave him?'

'They say they're going to pay it back.'

'I hope for her sake they do, poor woman.'

# THIRTY-TWO

Polly sat, gazing out of the café window. She sighed.

'That was a big sigh.'

'Just thinking.'

'Interesting.'

'How so much has changed in such a short space of time.'

'Well, you do like to keep busy.'

'A year ago I was working in a job which I hated, I was bossed around by Edna at the flower club.' She paused. 'Now I'm unemployed, I run my own flower club and have competed at the National Horticultural Show. And besides all that, I'm looking at setting up a cake company.'

'You never do things by halves, do you?'

'Not really.'

'So much for a quiet year. You were supposed to be taking things a lot easier since you don't have to work at the moment, but your redundancy payment won't last forever.'

'That's true. Perhaps I'll start earning a bit of money from my cake making.'

'You could always set yourself up as a private eye.' Mark laughed.

'Are you saying I'm nosy?'

'Ha ha. Your words, not mine. I'm just saying, you do like to find out what's happening in everyone's lives.'

'OK, OK. Sticking my nose into other people's business.'

'Well yes. You could put it that way.'

'I think I've had enough of that for one year. What with Angela and Suzy's husband. Freda's toy boy and the traumas of exhibiting at the National Horticultural Show.'

'I couldn't agree more. I'm not sure whether my nerves could take much more either,' laughed Mark.


The ladies were arriving at Polly's for an informal meeting.

'I thought it would be good for us to mark the first anniversary of our flower club and do a quick review of everything that's happened.'

'I can do that for you,' shouted Mark from the kitchen.

'No thank you. Just ignore him.' Polly knew what Mark was going to say.

'So, not only have we started our own club, which has been very successful, we have twenty-five members.'

'It's amazing how far we've come. After that first meeting I honestly wasn't sure if we'd get anyone to come back.'

'I think having the children's day helped,' Rose chipped in. She was determined to take credit for that idea, and in all honesty, it probably was the reason why more people started to attend the club meetings.

'Hold on a second. It looks like Maggie's just arriving.'

Polly glanced out of the lounge window and saw Maggie

parking her car, with a lot of shunting backwards and forwards to get into the tight space.

She looked a bit flustered when she came through the door.

'Everything OK, Maggie?'

'Yes. Well, no, actually. You know I live next door to Doris?'

'The little old lady?'

'Well, the dementia is getting worse.'

'What's she done now?' Polly and Sarah had heard many funny stories about this dear little lady who, due to dementia, had done some pretty crazy things in recent years.

'I persuaded her to get her food delivered. I was worried sick she might set fire to the house as she often forgot that she'd left a pan on the hob.'

'Or the kettle,' Lizzy reminded her.

'Yes, how could I forget the time we had to scrape melted plastic from her electric hob because she'd put the kettle on it to boil the water. This morning I heard our letterbox open, so I assumed the postman had been. Instead, I was greeted with the sight of spaghetti bolognaise all over the floor. Doris had it delivered for her lunch and didn't like it. She thought we might, so she posted it through our letterbox.'

'Oh my God!'

'It was everywhere. All over the new hall carpet.'

'It's not easy getting tomato stains out.'

'So we discovered.'

Polly was laughing. 'Tell everyone what happened the other day, you know, with the washing machine.'

'Oh yes. I popped round to check on her. She said she was fine. She was just putting the washing on. Next thing, there was a horrific crash. She'd only loaded the washing machine with her crockery.'

'Noo!' laughed Sarah. 'I suppose there was some logic there.'

'Exactly. The dishes needed washing so in Doris's mind, a washing machine was the most logical place to load her crockery. I had to ask Steve to go and help as I couldn't stop the cycle. Eventually he managed to get the door open. It took an age to get all the fragments of crockery out.'

'At least Steve was around to help.'

'Yes, but he hates going round to the house alone. Doris gets a bit fruity with him.'

'Really?'

'Yes, she's always on the lookout for a man. Some of the things she says are really X-rated.'

'What that dear little old lady?'

'The very one. The dementia has clearly switched off her inhibitions. The things she comes out with. The other day Steve had to go round there because she was so distressed. Apparently, a group of people had broken into her house and parked their car in her lounge. Steve had to pretend to tell them to leave and remove the car! Doris was so thrilled that he'd got rid of the intruders she wanted to give him a kiss. You can imagine Steve's reaction to that. When he came home he looked shell-shocked and insisted he never wanted to go round again!'

'We shouldn't laugh. Dementia is such a sad and dreadful illness.'

'Bless Doris. To her all of these situations and people are real. We do try to see the funny side of it.'

'Unless you've got spag bol all over your carpet.'

'Yes. Exactly.'

'Sorry to interrupt, but can we get back to the reason we're meeting today?' Whilst Maggie's story was interesting, Polly wanted to get back on track with the meeting.

'Sorry, did I interrupt your flow?'

'Not really. I just wanted to celebrate our first year and recap.'

'I'm still here, if you want me to recap for you?' called Mark, cheekily, from the kitchen.

'No, we don't, thanks. Just take a slice of cake and go, please,' laughed Polly.

'It's been one hell of a year. What with Freda and her toy boy. The saga of Derek/Daniel/David or whatever his name is and us doing the National Horticultural Show.' Polly had a point. It would have been impossible to have predicted what the year would bring. 'I can't believe you met someone who is worse than Edna,' exclaimed Lizzy.

'True. Who'd have thought it possible.' Polly laughed. She'd never met anyone quite as bad as Elizabeth.

'And what about Amy? Who'd have believed that by the end of the year we would like her?'

'I know. She's really nice once you get chatting to her. Not at all the stuck-up cow I thought she was.'

Polly had never really given her the opportunity to show her true colours until she had worked with her on the giant Ferris wheel.

'I wondered if we should ask her to join our committee.'

Lizzy almost choked on the sweet she had just put in her mouth. 'What?' she stuttered.

'Only joking. I just wanted to check if you were listening as you seemed more interested in the box of chocolates.'

'Thank goodness for that. I thought I was about to have a heart attack.'

'I thought I might have to do the Heimlich manoeuvre on you if you'd got that sweet stuck in your windpipe.'

'I think things are working well, just as we are,' claimed Rose, who was pleasantly surprised at how well the year had gone.

'So, who fancies a piece of my chocolate cake?'

'This isn't Edna's happy cake recipe, is it?'

Polly laughed, remembering the committee meeting when Edna had included some 'herbs' in a chocolate cake, not realising it was cannabis and she inadvertently managed to get the whole committee stoned.

'No. Not this time.'

She headed to the kitchen and picked up the cake. 'It's death by chocolate.' She laughed. 'Chocolate cake, chocolate frosting, chocolate decoration.'

'Blimey. Think I might have that heart attack after that.' Lizzy had a point.

'So how are the headaches? I thought you weren't allowed any chocolate.' Rose reminded Polly of the shocking results of a previous allergy test.

'Well, the bad news is that I'm still getting headaches. The good news is that it isn't chocolate that's causing them.' Polly cut herself a large slice of cake and sat down.

'I propose a toast.' Sarah held up her cup of tea. 'To the next twelve months. Let's hope they are as successful, although perhaps not as traumatic.'

# THIRTY-THREE

Freda was almost too afraid to open the email from Mo. She stared at it for ages, but eventually she took a deep breath and opened it. She needn't have worried as it was from the genuine Mo.

> Hello Freda
>
> I am so sorry what happened and hope you are OK. I have money to send you. It is not the full amount as that will take time to get but I want to send some money now. I hope you will forgive my uncle.

Freda felt sorry for Mo having to get involved. After all he was an innocent party too, but she was relieved that it looked like she'd get her money back at some stage. She phoned Rose to let her know.

'That's fabulous news. Mo seems like a lovely person, it's just a shame that his uncle decided to pretend to be him.'

Freda hadn't been able to face Edna since the fiasco at the

airport as she knew she would say, 'I told you so', but since she was now getting her money returned, she didn't feel such a fool. Rose continued to assure her that she had a lot of friends and should just ignore Edna or similar people who like to point out faults.

'You're always welcome to come and join Polly's flower club if you want to,' Rose had suggested. This seemed like a tempting offer as Freda was impressed at how supportive Polly, Sarah and Lizzy had been, especially at the airport.

'I'll think about it.' Freda didn't want to make the situation with Edna any worse. She knew the flower arranging world was very close knit and even if she joined Polly's club her path would still cross with Edna's at some point.

'How's Freda?'

'Not great. I think she's very embarrassed about what happened.' Edna's ears pricked up. 'Why, what happened?'

Rose looked at Lizzy, unsure whether or not to bring Edna up to date. 'Things didn't work out with her fella.'

'Just as I thought,' Edna sneered.

Rose glared at her. She really disliked Edna's smugness.

'Well, I'm just saying that it was highly unlikely a twenty-something would be interested in Freda.'

Whilst this sounded like a cruel comment, Rose and Lizzy had both had concerns too and knew that on this occasion, Edna was right.

'I'm assuming that's why she hasn't come to committee tonight.'

'Suppose so. I know she's very upset and shaken by the whole experience.'

'Well, she was a fool to send money to a complete stranger.' Edna's comment was totally heartless.

'Don't you think that comment is unnecessary? With hindsight that's true, but at the time Freda had no idea she was being scammed.'

'She can't hide away forever.'

'No, but she needs time to process all this, plus she's had her confidence knocked. She feels nervous all the time.'

'Instead of criticising her and saying how stupid she was, we should support her.'

Edna was never great at tea and sympathy and as things stood it was probably just as well.

'Poor Freda. I'll pop round tomorrow to see how she is.' Barbara had known Freda for years and tried to keep out of the discussions about her.

'Can we get on? I was wondering if we should consider having a flower show to try and bring in new members.'

Rose pulled a face. 'Do we think our members will participate?'

'I don't see why not. It's not a competition. Just a way to show off our skills and get other people interested in flower arranging.'

Barbara didn't speak. She'd learned to keep her head down when Edna was on a mission and looking for volunteers.

'Suppose so. I'm just worried we'll not have enough exhibits.'

'We can all do something, and I can think of at least another half a dozen who will.' Edna was confident that she could persuade her members.

Rose wasn't feeling quite as confident. She'd noticed that more and more members seemed to be dropping out or not wanting to participate in anything.

'I did wonder.' Edna hesitated for a second, 'if we could ask Polly if she'd like to join forces.'

Lizzy spluttered on a mouthful of tea and it came out of her nose.

'Are you OK, Lizzy?' asked Rose, feeling quite concerned.

'Did I hear you correctly?' She spluttered some more.

'Why not?'

'If we join forces we can have a lovely show. It could benefit all of us.'

'Actually, Edna, I think you might have a good idea. Polly's club has lots of enthusiastic members. I'm sure we can persuade some to have a go and enter something.'

Edna cringed at the mention of Polly's club. 'Would you ask her?'

'Who me? It's your idea, it might sound better coming from you.'

'I'm not sure how well Polly would receive me.'

'She'll be fine. Why not call her now?' Lizzy suggested, eager to be present for *that* conversation.

Edna wasn't so sure. 'Perhaps I'll call her later tonight.'

'No time like the present.' Rose pulled her phone from her bag and dialled Polly's number.

'Hello, Rose. Thought you were at committee tonight.'

'I am. Edna would like a word.' She passed the phone to a reluctant Edna.

'Hello, Polly. We've just been talking about holding a flower show and wondered if your club would like to join in.'

Polly was taken aback. She put her hand over her phone and whispered to Mark, 'Edna only wants to have a joint flower show.'

'Sounds like a great idea. Better than a craft show in London,' Mark enthused.

'That's true, but it's Edna.'

'And?'

'Are you still there, Polly?'

Lizzy wondered if Polly had fainted at the very suggestion that she hold a joint show with Edna.

'Yes. Why not?' Polly stuttered. 'Sounds like a good idea.'

'That's wonderful, Polly. I'll be in touch so we can plan it.'

Rose smiled. Pleased that perhaps this would smooth things over and get rid of the rivalry once and for all.

'Well, I never. You and Edna are working together. Who'd have thought it.' Mark couldn't believe his ears.

'Stop gloating, Mark. This might benefit us both.'

Edna felt pleased with hersself for being so magnanimous and putting aside her differences with Polly. That still didn't stop her from feeling slightly worried about the planning meeting with Polly.

'Just don't let Edna boss you about. This is a joint project,' warned Mark. He knew Polly only too well, but in recent months she'd become a lot more assertive, so he hoped there'd be a good outcome from her meeting with Edna.

They'd agreed to meet in "neutral" territory, the small café near Polly's just happened to sell the most delicious cakes.

Edna was already there when Polly arrived.

'Have you ordered?'

'No, I was waiting for you. I'm trying to decide which cake to try.'

Polly eyed the cakes. Her favourite lemon feather cake was there so it was an easy decision for her.

'That looks delicious,' noted Edna, 'but I'm not sure I could cope with that amount of cream. I think I'll try the coconut and raspberry cake.'

Polly began to relax as they entered into a conversation about cakes, the one major thing they had in common, along with some gossip.

'I still can't get over the day Lizzy crashed her car with all those cakes in it.' The story of her accident spread rapidly throughout the flower club.

Polly laughed. 'It was funny, although not for Lizzy. You should have seen the state of the cakes. All smashed up in the containers.'

'What a waste. I was wondering if we should have a cake stall at the flower show.'

Polly's ears pricked up. 'What, sell cakes?'

'Yes, we could charge an entry fee which includes a cup of tea and a slice of cake. Plus, they can buy cakes too. This should bring in quite a lot of money, to cover the cost of the hall etc. and perhaps give some funds to do some advertising.' Polly liked the sound of this.

She smiled. Mark was always having to remind her that this was supposed to be a flower club, not a cake club. Polly realised that she and Edna still had lots in common. 'Brilliant idea. I know a lot of ladies who I'm sure will enter a flower arrangement. Dare I suggest we could also have a child's category?'

'Oh, OK.' Edna wasn't so sure.

'We had a children's day and it proved to be very successful. Although there was quite a mess left behind and the children seemed to be on a sugar high after eating loads of cakes.'

Edna roared with laughter. Another thing she had in common with Polly was that she wasn't overly fond of children at the best of times, but perhaps on this occasion this might be a good idea.

'Everyone could bring in their designs ready-made so we don't have loads of mess.'

'Good idea. What theme should we have?'

'How about musicals? Everyone likes musicals or has at least seen one.'

'The children could do a nursery rhyme. Do you think children still have nursery rhymes?' Edna wasn't too sure what the latest trend was.

'Not sure, I think it might be digital games nowadays.' Polly realised that she really had no idea what children liked either. 'How about a favourite cartoon or superhero?'

'Sounds a better idea to me.' Edna was pleased that Polly had some good ideas. 'So, we're settled. I'll confirm some dates with the vicar and will get back to you. How was your cake?'

'Delicious as always, though I don't think I could eat any more. What about you?'

'That was delicious too. Perhaps I'll try to make one for our flower show.' Both ladies left the meeting feeling good about the show and well and truly stuffed.

# THIRTY-FOUR

'Polly, would you come with me to choose a new car?' asked Lizzy. The insurance had finally paid out.

'Oh, Lizzy. I don't know the first thing about cars. So long as it has four tyres and an engine that's fine for me.'

Lizzy laughed. 'Me too, but I'd really appreciate your opinion.'

When Polly told Mark, he laughed. 'What? But you don't know anything about cars.'

'That's exactly what I told Lizzy.'

'Talk about the blind leading the blind.'

Polly drove over to Lizzy's where she was anxiously waiting. It was a short drive to the garage. On the forecourt, shining and gleaming was the car Lizzy had fallen in love with.

'Isn't it lovely? I always wanted a red car.'

'Yes, but does it go?'

'No idea. We'll soon find out.'

'Hello, ladies.' The young sales assistant bounded over to them, eager to make his first sale of the day.

After unlocking the car, Lizzy stroked the seats. 'It feels lovely.' She was in ecstasy.

Polly could see that Lizzy was sold on the car, regardless of whether or not it was a good buy.

'Can we take it out for a test run?' asked Polly, in an attempt to give the impression she wasn't sold just on the colour of the car and luxurious interior.

'You're welcome to take it out for a drive.'

'Just the two of us?'

'Sure. I don't need to come with you. We can put madam on our insurance.'

Polly suddenly felt her tummy sink. The thought of letting Lizzy loose with someone else's car scared her, especially as she would be the passenger.

The sales assistant collected the keys and ran through some basic instructions, although Polly could tell Lizzy wasn't paying much attention at all. They set off at a reasonably slow pace whilst Lizzy negotiated the traffic. *It's running smoothly enough*, noted Polly, still gripping onto the seat belt in case Lizzy made a sudden stop. They pulled into a quiet road and stopped.

'I love it, I love it.' Lizzy was beaming.

'I know you do. It seems really great.' Polly couldn't help the slight pang of jealousy at the thought of Lizzy having such a lovely car.

'Let's sit in the back to see how much legroom there is.'

They both got out and climbed into the back.

'Not bad. It's very comfortable, with a decent amount of legroom. And there's plenty of space for "stuff" if I put the seats down.'

'Let's go back and tell him you'll have it.'

Lizzy beamed. 'Oh yes.'

Polly tried the door. It wouldn't open.

'I can't get out.'

Lizzy tried her door. 'Neither can I. I bet they've got the bloody child locks on.'

'Are you telling me we're stuck in here?'

'What are we going to do?'

Lizzy started banging on the window in panic.

'There's no one around.'

'We're going to have to climb into the front and open the driver's door.'

Lizzy managed to crouch on the rear seat but couldn't get her leg through the gap between the seats. 'I can't do it. You try.'

Polly doubted she'd fare any better as she was hardly athletic but thought she'd give it a go. After several attempts she found herself straddled most uncomfortably between the back and front seats.

'I'm stuck. I can't go either way now.' She could feel herself panicking.

'Can you reach my phone?' asked Lizzy. Polly stretched as far as she could and managed to flick Lizzy's phone from the dashboard onto the floor. Lizzy positioned herself so she could just about reach it.

'Phew, got it.'

'Phone Mark,' ordered Polly. She couldn't see the funny side of the situation and feared they could be stuck for hours.

Lizzy did as instructed and put the phone on speaker.

'Hello, Lizzy. What's up?'

'We're stuck,' shouted Polly.

'What do you mean, you're stuck? Where are you?'

'We're in Lizzy's new car and I'm stuck between the backseats and front.'

'You what?'

'You heard.'

'What on earth are you doing there?'

'We sat in the back to see what it's like and the child locks are on so we're trapped.'

Mark couldn't control his laughter. Tears were streaming down his face. 'You're supposed to sit in the front seat to drive a car. Didn't they tell you that at your driving test?'

'Never mind that.' Polly was getting annoyed and desperate. She wished she'd gone to the loo before she'd left home, *and* her leg that was trapped was beginning to cramp up.

'Can you get here urgently?'

'OK where are you?'

'We left the garage and turned left,' replied Lizzy.

'No, we didn't, we turned right and then left.'

'You sure? I thought we turned left.'

'Don't worry about it. I'll find you.' He sensed this discussion could go on for ages as they both had a habit of getting lost and had a dreadful sense of direction at the best of times. 'I'll track Polly's phone. See you soon. Oh, what car are you in?'

'A red one. You can't miss it. It's a red car with two women trapped inside,' Polly replied, sarcastically.

'See you soon.'

It had only been about ten minutes but felt like hours to Polly. By the time Mark had tracked them down the windows were all steamed up. He opened the front passenger door. 'Hello!' He burst out laughing, pointed his phone and took a photo.

'Don't you dare.'

'We've got to have a record of this.' He snapped away.

'MARK! Will you hurry up? I need the loo.'

He opened the back passenger door to allow Lizzy to leave the car.

Getting Polly out was going to prove a more challenging task since she was jammed between the front and back seats.

'If I support your front, can you get your legs into the back?'

Polly tried. 'No, I'm well and truly stuck.'

'Can I help at all?' came a voice over Mark's shoulder. Standing there was Rod, the firefighter who had delivered Polly's cake tins back to her following Lizzy's accident.

He recognised Lizzy, although he didn't recognise Polly.

'I'm stuck. Can someone just get me out please,' screamed Polly.

Rod looked at Mark, noticing the tears of mirth in his eyes. 'Just don't ask, mate.' Mark was trying to control his laughter but was failing miserably.

'If you go in the back and unhook her leg, I will pull her out from the front.'

'You're joking!'

'Well, it's either that or I get the lads from the station and we take the roof off.'

Lizzy turned pale. 'No please don't do that. I'm only test driving it. I haven't bought it yet, and I love it.' She had visions of a fire engine arriving and a team of firefighters cutting the car to pieces just to get Polly out.

Rod laughed. 'I was only kidding. On three. One, two, three.' Mark pushed Polly's leg, while Rod pulled her arms and with a completely over-the-top scream from Polly, she was free.

She stood on the pavement beside the car.

'Don't you *ever* ask me to come for a test drive with you again.' Now she was free she was starting to see the funny side of the situation.

'Before you go, I'll take the child locks off so you don't get stuck again,' informed Rod.

'Thanks so much. Once again, you've come to the rescue.' Polly felt a bit embarrassed.

'Sorry I didn't recognise you from the other angle – nice to see you again. The cakes you gave us were delicious.'

'Are you both sure you're safe to drive back to the garage? Can I go home and get on with my work?' Mark felt reluctant to leave them on their own.

'Yes, of course we are.'

They drove in silence, relieved that the ordeal was over. By the time they arrived at the garage, the salesman was looking decidedly concerned.

'Thank goodness you're back. I wondered if you'd done a runner or had an accident.'

'No,' replied Polly abruptly. 'Anyway, you had my car as collateral.'

'Not wishing to insult you but I don't think *that* car could be classed as collateral.'

'How rude,' Polly huffed. 'We had a bit of a problem, but all is well now.'

'So, how did you get on with the car? Do you like it?'

'Absolutely. I want to buy it.'

'What, even after the drama we had?'

'Yes. I love it. I just don't think I'll sit in the back again.'

The salesman looked bemused.

'It's a long story,' laughed Polly, shaking her head.

# THIRTY-FIVE

Mark didn't dare comment on the number of cake tins Polly had piled up in the hall. He'd learnt not to challenge her and had deliberately stayed away from the kitchen for the last few days. Not that he could have got in there had he wanted to as every surface was covered in something, whether it was baking equipment, cooling cakes or a sticky surface of icing sugar.

'Need any help loading up the car?'

Polly was struggling with packing everything in. She nodded. 'Please, Mark. I think the cake tins first, then my flower arrangements.'

Sarah arrived at a crucial moment. 'Do you want me to take some? Looks like you're really loaded up.'

'That would be great, thanks.'

Sarah looked at Mark and smiled. They were both thinking the same thing about the amount of stuff Polly was trying to squeeze into her car. Mark loaded a number of tins into Sarah's car.

When they arrived at the church hall, they were both

relieved to see Edna was already there giving out orders to the caretaker.

'Poor man,' laughed Sarah.

'Yes, but at least we don't have to put all the tables up.'

The hall was set up with tables for the exhibits and even more for the cakes. In fact, there were enough cakes to open a bakery.

'Wonderful,' Edna enthused as Polly brought in the seemingly never-ending stream of cake containers. Even she wondered if they'd gone a bit overboard with their baking. 'What a fabulous selection of cakes.'

Polly could see the funny side of it. Perhaps Mark was right. If you didn't know any better you'd think this was a cake show.

'Just hope lots of people turn up.'

During the course of the morning ladies from both flower clubs turned up with their flower arrangements. There was quite an array of colours and styles.

By the time the show officially opened the hall was filled with the wonderful scent of flowers and cakes. Polly was manning the cake table and doing a roaring trade.

Edna was busy organising the tea and coffee whilst Barbara and Freda ran round the kitchen topping up kettles and teapots.

'I never thought I'd see this day.'

'What day?'

'Polly and Edna working together after everything that was said.'

'Well, perhaps pigs do fly after all.'

'They both look to be enjoying themselves.'

'Yes. But I doubt they'd admit to that.'

Maggie arrived. 'I thought I'd bring Doris along. You know, my neighbour.'

Lizzy smiled. 'Oh yes. Lovely to see you.' She took Maggie to one side.

'I hope you're going to keep an eye on her.'

'Don't worry. I've got it all under control.'

Maggie had worried about taking Doris along to the show but thought it would be a nice afternoon out for her as she rarely went anywhere these days.

'Who's that with Maggie?' Polly was curious.

'That's her neighbour, Doris. You know, the spag bol affair.'

Polly laughed. 'I hope we don't have any problems with her.'

'Maggie insists she's got the situation under control.'

It was rare that Mark attended anything to do with flowers, but he felt Polly would appreciate his support at this joint venture. He was usually involved in fetching and carrying but the temptation of a slice of Polly's triple chocolate cake had been the decider.

He'd barely walked into the hall before he was accosted by Doris.

'Mathew? I knew it was you. My. You haven't changed a bit.'

Mark looked bemused. 'I think you've mistaken me for someone else.'

'No, I haven't. Don't tease.' She linked her arm in his and gave it a squeeze.

Fortunately, Maggie wasn't far away. 'Mathew was Doris's boyfriend when she was in her twenties,' she whispered to

Mark. 'Just go along with it. It would break Doris's heart if I told her you're not him.'

Mark smiled, albeit uneasily.

Doris squeezed his arm again and whispered sweet nothings in his ear. Mark blushed.

Polly caught his eye as he mouthed the word, 'Help.'

'Can you cover for a minute? I think I need to rescue Mark.'

'Sure. He does look a bit flustered.'

'What's up?'

'Doris thinks I'm her old boyfriend. You should hear some of the things she said. What she wants to do with me. It's quite embarrassing.'

Polly sniggered. 'She's eighty-nine years old.'

'I don't think that would stop her.'

'Maggie, could you keep Doris under control? She's just hit on Mark.'

'I know she has. Wait until I tell Steve he's got a rival. He thought he was Doris's toy boy.'

'Is she enjoying the show?'

'Yes, she's loving it. I'm so pleased to see her having a good time, but I've just had to rescue a piece of your chocolate fudge cake from her handbag. She'd decided to take it home for later.'

'That's no problem, she can take a piece.'

'Not stuffed in the pocket of her bag.'

'No, I see what you mean.'

'I just wiped the chocolate frosting off her bus pass as it was covered in it.'

'Perhaps we'd better keep her away from the cakes then.'

'Also, it's been a bit embarrassing as she's been giving her opinion on the arrangements in a rather loud voice.'

'Oh dear.'

'Indeed. Funny how the censor is switched off when you have dementia. I've had to rush her past one or two of the designs that I thought she'd have an opinion on.'

As fast as Polly sold a cake, another person was queuing. Sarah was desperately trying to keep up with making up cardboard cake boxes for Polly to put the cakes in.

'Uh oh. Angela and Suzy are here. With their kids.'

'Move the cakes away from the edge. I don't want Sebastian and Luke sticking their fingers in them.'

Sebastian made a beeline for the cake stand.

'Look, Mummy, chocolate cake.' His finger reached across the table, but Sarah managed to get to the cake before he did and move it to a safe distance.

'Hello, they look lovely.'

'Don't forget your entry fee covers tea and cake.' Polly reminded them as she steered them in Edna's direction. She smiled inwardly wondering how Edna was going to deal with the situation. As they approached the serving hatch Edna was busy dispensing cakes. She looked horrified as a grubby little finger appeared on the counter and touched one of the cakes.

'Is that the one you'd like?' she asked Sebastian rather abruptly.

'No, I want one of those.' He pointed to another cake on the opposite side of the counter. 'Well, you've touched this one now so that's the one you've got to have.'

'Mummy.' Tears started welling up in his eyes and he was on the brink of throwing a tantrum.

'Don't worry. I'll have that one and you can have a chocolate one.' Angela decided to let him have his own way. She was in no mood for a tantrum.

Suzy appeared at the counter with Luke. He began to kick the leg of the counter.

'Excuse me, young man.' Edna peered over the counter at him. Luke ignored her and continued kicking the counter. 'Stop doing that, Luke,' shouted Suzy. Luke started to cry.

Since Derek's double life had come to light the situation had been tough on Angela and Suzy, but especially on the children. Sharing a husband wasn't the easiest relationship in the world, especially as Derek often messed up the plans, claiming to have forgotten he 'had to work late', whatever that meant.

Luke stretched his arm onto the counter and stuck his finger in one of the chocolate cakes that was close to hand. 'I want this one,' he demanded.

'No. You're not having a whole cake. You can share one with me.' Suzy said to him. 'He's so hyper at the moment. The last thing I want is him running around,' she said to Edna.

*That's the last thing I want too*, thought Edna. She handed over the cake and let out a sigh of relief. Polly could see she was unimpressed.

'See you've met the terrible twins.'

'Oh. I didn't realise they were related. I thought they had different mothers.'

'Well, they are as good as twins. They both have the same father.'

Edna raised her eyebrows.

'Neither woman knew that either until a recent chance meeting.'

'What a dirty rotter.'

'My feelings exactly.'

'But the women are friends?'

'Yes, and they've got an arrangement with the dad to look after the kids.'

'Well, I never. This would never have happened in my day.'

'I bet it did. Just that everyone kept things behind closed doors then. Nowadays everyone is open about relationships.'

'True. I suppose you have a point.' Edna perused the room and noticed all the people admiring the flower arrangements or buying cake. She beamed. 'I think we should give ourselves a pat on the back, Polly. We definitely work well as a team.'

For once Polly agreed with her. Perhaps they weren't in competition with each other after all, but two people on the same side, working to a common goal.

'I'm so proud of you, Polly.' Mark came up behind her, put his arms around her and whispered in her ear. 'I knew you could pull this off. There's no point in fighting. Life is tough enough, and you know, when it comes down to it, it really is only a bunch of flowers.'

Polly turned and pecked Mark on the cheek. 'I knew you were going to say that and for once I'm going to agree with you. It is just a bunch of flowers, and I might add, a piece of cake.'